Sturgeon's West

Sturgeon's West

By THEODORE STURGEON
and DON WARD

DOUBLEDAY & COMPANY, INC.

GARDEN CITY, NEW YORK

All of the characters in this book are fictitious, and any resemblance to actual persons, living or dead, is purely coincidental.

ISBN: 0-385-05393-2
Library of Congress Catalog Card Number 73–135717

CONTENTS

Sturgeon's West

Ted Sturgeon's Western Adventure

When I suggested to a leading practitioner of science-fiction and fantasy that he write a Western story little did I suspect what would result. As I remember, I had small hope that a positive response would ensue. But it did, and it kept on happening from time to time—and now the happenings have made a book, *Sturgeon's West*.

At the time I was editing *Zane Grey's Western*, a monthly magazine that enjoyed a substantial acceptance among the followers of the genre. I was also an enthusiastic reader of science-fiction. One night I read a wondrous tale, "Maturity," and its author was Theodore Sturgeon. I liked the humor and the significance, and, above all, the sheer humanity of it, so much that I wrote a letter to Sturgeon. I told him how much I enjoyed "Maturity" and made that suggestion, wistfully—it would be a special pleasure for *ZGW* readers if he would do a story with some of those elements for that magazine.

It brought a quick and grateful letter from Ted—one that made me even more of a fan of his than his story already had. And, several weeks later, the mail brought to my desk a Western story by Theodore Sturgeon: "Well Spiced."

That letter and that story initiated a long enduring friendship and made the start of a modest but I think significant contribution to the field of Western fiction. After "Well Spiced" came the little gem of a story called "Scars" and after that there was "Cactus Dance," which is the only Sturgeon Western that has an element of the fantastic.

For a while after that it seemed that the corpus of Sturgeon's Western writing would comprise those three stories and no more. ZGW, one of the last Western magazines to fall before the rising challenge of the TV horse opera, went the way of the others. The market for Western short stories vanished.

Together, Ted and I found an alternate route to publication. In collaboration (my contribution minor, his major) we produced "The Waiting Thing Inside" and "The Man Who Figured Everything," both of which came out in *Ellery Queen's Mystery Magazine*—Westerns though they indubitably are ("Western Crime Stories," I think editor Fred Dannay called them). Rounding out this collection are two hitherto unpublished tales, "Ride In, Ride Out" and "The Sheriff of Chayute."

Of this last named group, Ted and I point with modest pride to the fact that "The Waiting Thing Inside" won an honorable mention in one of *EQMM*'s annual prize story competitions. The magazine's editorial comment accompanying "The Man Who Figured Everything" noted that it not only shattered the main conventions of the standard Western (intentionally) but also those of mystery-story writing (presumably unintentionally). Anyway it got into print—maybe for those reasons—and a lot of readers liked it.

On the other hand, "Ride In, Ride Out" never won acceptance by a magazine publisher although we agree it's the best of our collaborative efforts. We are pretty happy that at last it's getting an airing here.

It has been an exciting adventure, Ted Sturgeon's Western one. Many thanks for bringing me along on that ride, Ted. And even more for the friendship that has lasted over the years . . .

That one of the greatest of all our s-f writers has given us these stories to add to the wide and varied range of the Western is, I think, cause for some literary amen-saying.

Let's do it again, Ted.

DON WARD

Well Spiced

THEODORE STURGEON

Tamarisk just happened. Some forgotten Conestoga cap'n
had chosen the Tamarisk hollow as a route down the valley,
rather than the exactly similar hollow on the other side of
the rise. The town's first building appeared when one Pericles Zapappas sold the oxen which hauled his chuck wagon.
The old wagon, hub-deep in the sandy soil, was the nucleus.
Because it was there, it was logical to set up a general sup-
plies shack near it, and because of the shack and its increas-
ing stock, settlers took to the nearby lush foothills, knowing
they had a trading place. With the settlers came the helpers
and the hangers-on, the blacksmiths and the gamblers, the
assay office and the livery stable and the hotel.

Pericles Zapappas stuck with Tamarisk. He hadn't planned
to; he hadn't planned not to. It was just that there were so
many people to feed—and he liked feeding people. He liked
to see the tin plates, and later, the thick china ones, mopped
clean with great chunks of sourdough bread, or the muscular black loaves he baked himself. The old wagon soon
sported a canvas awning which became a mess tent which
gradually acquired wooden walls and a tin roof, and as the
busy years and the busy wagon trains passed, there was a
new building with a real kitchen, rows of iron skillets, three
glass sugar bowls, and a spittoon.

Pericles was the only fixture that showed no change. He was a grizzled, tubby little man, with a complexion the color of a frankfurter and a skin like a silk pillow slip that has been slept on for three hot nights. His eyes were round, clear, and blue, giving the impression of red-hot portholes into an ice box. He smiled often, never laughed, and was always a little frightened—afraid that the meat wouldn't arrive, that the coffee would boil, that a customer wasn't getting enough to eat. He absorbed insults and compliments with the same gentle smile and the same shuffling backward retreat, as from royalty.

Tamarisk was good to live in, as such places go, when the wind was from the hills. But when it came panting up from the desert with fire and salt on its breath, the town shimmered and crackled and dried in it. It was on such a day that Fellows stamped into Pericles's place, and the youth's language was not one whit less blistering than the desert wind. His profanity swirled in, all but sweeping Pericles off his precarious perch on a serving table, where he was hanging mesh bags of garlic, strings of melon rind, and chains of herbs and barks to dry; for Pericles was a great hand in the spice department.

"Feed me!" roared Fellows. "By God, likker won't do fer this. Gimme some o' that slumgullion of yours, the kind that wallops you hot an' then smooths you off easy."

Pericles climbed down and framed the kid in his round blue stare. "Hey boy. Whatsa do—burn down you stable?"

"It's thet money-jinglin' Eastern toad, Barstow," spat the youngster. "Him an' his gunmen an' his 'fer th' good of th' country'!"

"Meest' Barstow is crazy," said Pericles mildly. "Tamarisk

is a plenty big town for the valley. Whats 'e wan' for to make a new one?"

Fellows folded himself into a creaky chair, knocking his holster clear so that it swung as he sat. "Jest why he's don' it don't worry me right now. It's whut he's doin'. You know what he done? He started a livery stable over there. He ain't got but four hosses, an' nothing but a drunked-up ol' prospector to care for'm. But he's *givin'* 'em away! I can't charge a ranny prices like thet! Feed costs me, Peri, thet an' a hand to guard the place at night, what with hoss thieves an' fire an' all."

Pericles, well within earshot, stirred his spices into the witches' brew he called slumgullion. "Meest' Barstow dig a well," he called.

"Yeh. I heerd about thet. Whut's he aim to git from it—tamarisk roots?"

Pericles, tipping some of the precious fluid from a carboy mounted on a pivoted frame, grunted, "Water, Fellows. He got it, also."

"You mean to tell me he struck water over there?"

"He got town well. Cab Jenks, this man with piebal' gelding, he come tell me this morning."

"Oh," said Fellows, and it was an eloquent syllable. There was a recess for thinking, and then he said, "Peri, if he's got water, it ain't no good for Tamarisk."

"Yes," said Pericles. "No good."

"What's Tamarisk?" Fellows burst out after a troubled silence. "So many shacks, so many people—what the hell. Let it go. It might's well be a ghost town, like Harriston or DuMoulin's Gulch."

"Yes," said Pericles, coming around the partition with a deep, steaming bowl of stew. "But—we build Tamarisk. You,

you stable. Me, my place. Gomez an' he saddles. Trask an'
he cotton goods. Rogers an' Hark an' that ol' fella Mickey
Mack. Hm?"

"Yeh, Peri—but a *well!* We ain't got no well. We dug for'm
twice, an' you know what we got. Sweat, not water. We
got to haul water a mile and a half from Feegan's Brook."
He dug into the stew as if he hated it, which he did not.
"How'd he know he'd strike water there?" he demanded
with his mouth full. "Builds six shacks," he growled—quite
an achievement through that much stew, "an' suddenly hits
water in country where they ain't a water hole in ten miles,
'cept where the desert drinks up Feegan's Brook."

"What's about the spring, Fellows?"

"Spring? Oh—thet. Yeah. Four miles over the other way.
Whyn't he build his town over by there, if he had to build a
town?"

Pericles smiled—the smile he used instead of a laugh.
"Spring in the cliff. What trade he get by there? Bighorns?
Rock squirrels?"

"I see what you mean. His place and Tamarisk sit smack
in the middle of the only two trade routes through here. Aw,
mebbe you're right, Peri. Maybe he's jest crazy."

"Ask him," said Pericles, in a slightly awed voice.

"Huh?" Fellows's startled eyes swung from the Greek
around to the door, which was being blocked at the moment
by several cubic feet of flabby flesh, girdled by a too-new
cartridge belt and topped with a city-made Stetson. "Barstow!"

"Good morning, good morning," said the heavy man,
laughing what had been described as a diddling laugh, "and
how are the thriving burghers of Tamarisk today?"

Fellows put down his spoon and hooked his thumbs in

his belt, the fingers of his left hand sliding down to check the gentle swinging of his holster. His eyes were like cracks in a board as he took the Easterner's measure.

Barstow looked him up and down and turned a broad and insulting back. "Mr. Zapappas," he said unctuously. "Ahh. You're looking well this morning. How's business?"

Pericles sidled behind a counter. He regarded Barstow without his smile. "Business always good."

"Splendid, splendid," said Barstow heartily. "Glad to hear it. Make the best of it while it lasts, I always say." Then there was that laugh again. Suddenly he turned to Fellows—so suddenly that the youngster dropped his spoon and cursed viciously, "And how is the livery business?"

"Good, no thanks to you," snarled Fellows.

"Hey, Fellows, make no trouble in my place, huh?"

Barstow tittered. "There won't be any trouble, Mr. Zapappas," he said. "Mr. Fellows is not familiar with—ah—modern business methods. Now, if he would like to take over my stable, perhaps—"

"I'd jest as soon go back to ridin' fence," said Fellows evenly.

"That's good! Ha ha! that's very good. Young man, by the time Tamarisk is a ghost city, I'll own all the fences hereabouts, and you'll have to travel many a dry mile before you can hire out without my permission. Ha ha! Better come in with me while you can. I could use a good—"

"Y' won't use me," snapped Fellows.

Barstow shrugged, as if the movement were sufficient to send Fellows into limbo and beyond, and turned back to the Greek. "It so happens, Mr. Zapappas, that there is no eating place in Well City at the moment."

"What's you say, Well City?"

"Ah, yes, yes indeed. Well City it is, and Well City it will be. Ha! The very name shows that it has a future. Tamarisk! That's all anyone could expect to find here—desert greens. Now, in Well City, there's water—good, pure water."

"I heard," said Fellows, looking out at the rolling desert and its clumps of tamarisk.

Barstow ignored him, to hang his belly on the edge of the counter. "Now, Mr. Zapappas—surely we can come to some agreement on a catering-establishment in Well City."

Pericles shook his head with such timidity that the gesture was a mere quiver of wattles.

"Now, now," said Barstow heartily, "at least come over to look us over. Well City's going to be a great little place. I'm wrong. Well City *is* a great little place. A foresighted businessman—"

"Ef it's so nice yonder," drawled Fellows, "why don't you go on back to it?"

Pericles recognized the tone. It reminded him vividly of his dislike of the smell of gun smoke indoors and its attendant corpses. He opened his mouth, closed it, opened it again and said, "Sure. Sure, Meest' Barstow. Tomorrow."

Barstow brought his hands together with a meaty crash and scrubbed them happily against each other. "Splendid, Mr. Zapappas. Splendid. You shall have the—ha!—keys to the city. A good day to you, sir." He strode to the door, turned and stared coldly at Fellows. "As for you, young man, it will pay you to remember that the law is loaded heavier than that pop-gun of yours."

Fellows emitted a .45-caliber oath and sprang up, clawing at his hip. Pericles yelped as if burned, and by the time Fellows had looked at him and back to the door, Barstow was gone.

"Peri," said Fellows menacingly, "you are a traitor. You ain't really goin' to go over to thet—Well City tomorrow?"

"I think yes," said Pericles faintly but firmly, his eyes on Fellows's gun hand. "Hey, finish you stew."

"Thet Barstow walked out o' here with my appetite," grumbled the youngster. He threw a leg over his chair and sat down with an elbow on each side of his bowl. The spicy vapors of the stew curled into his angry nostrils, and he began to shovel tentatively, but shoveling, nevertheless. It took three spoonfuls to fill his mouth, whereupon he said, "Whut's this law ol' frog-face is talkin' about?"

Pericles frowned worriedly. "Big talk."

"It's more'n thet," said Fellows grudgingly. "He's mighty cocky to be bluffin'. Y' reckon he's on to somethin' we don't know?"

At last Pericles smiled. "Soon we know," he said. "Tomorrow. Hm?"

Fellows glanced up as the light dawned in his brain. "Peri, you got somethin' up your sleeve, or stuck in your boot. I know you, you greasy ol' son-of-a-gun. Whut you aimin' to do over there tomorrow?"

"Spice a little, stir a lot," said Pericles happily, using his stock answer to questions about his cooking.

It was late the following afternoon that Pericles's flea-bitten mare plodded wearily up to the restaurant. Fellows was standing in the shade, leaning back and whittling. He stepped out and caught the bridle, holding it while the little man dismounted heavily.

"Hot," said Pericles unnecessarily.

"It is thet," said Fellows, throwing the reins over the rail. "Hey, Peri—whut's the idea o' them oversize saddlebags? Whut'd you tote over there—a month's grub?"

Pericles ignored the question, mopping his crinkled face. "Well City very busy," he said.

"Is, huh?"

They went inside. "Plenty fellas driving stakes," wheezed the Greek. "Marking streets. Meest' Barstow show me everyt'ing. Place for courthouse, place for smithy, place for hotel and dance hall."

"Holy smoke! What's he think he's doin'?"

Pericles knelt to kindle the stove. "Place for depot too."

"*Depot?* Depot for what? Pony Express?"

Pericles shook his head. "Meest' Barstow, he tells me the big secret. Railroad coming through the Valley."

Fellows, poised over a chair, said "Ah-*hah!*" sitting heavily with the second syllable. "So thet's whut th' horned toad is after. Finds out they're runnin' a railroad survey through here, buys up some desert from the Federal Gov'm'nt, stakes out a town, and sits in it ontil th' railroad goes through." He clapped his hand to his head and moaned, "An' he has to go and find hisself a well. Hey—Peri! How about thet? D'you see it?"

"I see it. Meest' Barstow, first thing gives me a drink water from it. Pull up the bucket himself. Pour it like he think it's beer. All morning, want me for drink more."

"So he's really got water in his town, huh? Oh, thet ain't good, Peri."

"Not good. Well right in the middle of town."

"Yeah. I c'n see whut's goin' to happen to us an' Tamarisk when Well City gits to be a rail town." He shook his head. "No wonder Barstow took a day showin' you around."

"No all day. I took a ride," said Pericles cryptically. He went to the door and looked out toward the rise and Well City. "Fellows."

"Huh?"

"You know what? I never learn to load six-gun like yours."

"Well, I'll be—I never knowed you was interested. You don't never carry a gun." His eyes narrowed. "You expectin' trouble, Peri?"

Pericles shrugged. He looked up at the rise again. There was a feather of dust at its lip. "Show me, Fellows."

"Why shore." Fellows slipped the plated hogleg out of its holster. "Ain't nothin' to it. You pull this back, break it like this, an' jest slip your ca'tridges in these here holes."

"Whats about this thing. What you call? Cylinder?"

"Thet? It spins a little each time you shoot. You know thet."

"If it jams? Why, thet's easy enough. With the gun broke like this, the cylinder lifts right out. See? Then you can rod the holes out."

Pericles reached for the cylinder, his bright eyes glinting as his hand closed on it. "I see. Fellows—*look!*"

The youngster followed Pericles's pudgy finger. Down over the rise swept a group of horsemen.

"Wh— Hey, they're from Well City! That's Barstow's crew!" He spun back to the Greek, who had moved behind the partition, where his concoctions were beginning to steam and simmer on the stove. Fellows skidded around the counter and into the rear. "Peri! I don't know how much you know about this, but those guys are loaded for bear. What's goin' on?"

At Fellows's first shout, Pericles had started elaborately, and was now staring dismally into one of the pots. "Hey, boy. You shout too much with you mouth. Now look what happen, I drop you dirty cylinder into my stew."

"You what? Why, you galoot! Thet thing—"

The Well City posse swept past, thirty strong, whooping.
There were one or two shots. Fellows cursed, scooped up
his gun, and ran for the door. Pericles smiled radiantly,
sounded the stew with a wooden spoon, and delicately
fished out the cylinder. He carefully washed it and dried it,
and put it in the cash drawer.

Twenty minutes later he was busily packing liquor bottles
into a crate with straw. There was the rustling beat of hoofs
on the hard-packed street, and the posse streamed past,
bunched around two riders with dispatch cases.

Fellows pounded in, his face scarlet from the effort to
exude profanity and take in air simultaneously. "Peri!
Gimme my — ––– cylinder while I fill their — ––––s full
o' ––– lead!"

"Whatsa do?"

" 'Whatsa do?' " screamed Fellows, dancing as if his chaps
were full of fire ants. "Don't ask me questions, damn yuh!
I'm mad enough at your clumsiness. You done cass-trated
my hawglaig. Now don't make me madder by actin' foolish."

Pericles glanced out at the rise, where the posse was
dwindling out of gunshot. He moved to the cash drawer, set
the cylinder on the counter, and scrambled in quivering
panic away from Fellows's wild dive for it. The kid punched
it into his gun, rammed home some shells, and bolted for the
door. The sight of the posse pouring over the top of the hill
and out of sight deflated him to the point where his shoulders seemed to dislocate. He went completely limp except
for his jaw muscles. He made no sound.

Pericles smiled. "You cuss too much," he observed. "An'
when you get real mad, you got not'ing left to say. Hm?"

Fellows turned slowly, slowly raised his fists to his cartridge belt, and treated Pericles to a glare that would have dried up an oat-fed cow with a three-day calf.

Pericles turned pale. "Want a cup coffee?" he murmured.

Fellows ignored the suggestion, while Pericles bustled himself pouring the coffee into a mug. "Peri, you are jest too good-hearted an' stupid to stay alive. Don't you know what them rannies jest did?"

"Whatsa do?"

"I'll tell you 'whatsa do,'" rasped the youngster. "Surrounded the marshal's office, that's what, where ol' Mickey Mack keeps all the town records. They got all them papers and rid off with 'em before anybody in town knew which way to jump." He tapered off to a trickling, inarticulate mumble which returned in another flood of unprintables.

When the noise had died down again, Pericles asked mildly, "Was it legal?"

"Legal? Whaddeya mean legal? It was kidnapin', that's what the hell! Oh, they poked some papers at Mickey Mack fust—"

"What kind papers?"

"I dunno. Mickey tol' us—me and Hark and some more that was there. Somepin' about Well City bein' a county seat, an' a seizure order fer th' county records f'm the marshal's office at Topeka. So what's that?" He snorted. "Them was our records, Tamarisk records—all the deeds an' claims an' transfer notes an' all. What's Well City want with 'em?"

"It was legal," said Pericles quietly. Fellows sat while that sank in. Pericles put coffee before him and said, "It was legal, even if it was no good, boy. Your gun makes big noise, big trouble. Barstow, he say the law is loaded heavier'n you are. Is right."

"Why, you interferin' ol' belly-stuffer!" bawled Fellows. "You spiked my gun thet a way a-purpose!"

"Please," Pericles whispered out of a dry throat. His face was puckered with terror, for Fellows was three degrees uglier than just formidable when his dander soared. "Fellows. Please, boy. Hey. No make trouble in my place. Drink you coffee. You right. Meest' Barstow tell me about this county seat business. Federal judge, he give charter because of well. No use to tell you—you get mad, all you sense run out you mouth, you shoot and then you hang. No good. Well City is county seat. Is legal."

"They cain't do this!" wailed Fellows. "All this country here was settled out o' Tamarisk! Then this Easterner walks off with the rail line an' th' county records and sits down on desert he bought fer nothin' and can sell fer a mint!"

"Is the business methods he talk about."

"It's the business, all right," gritted Fellows, and added something about Barstow that would have been shocking in Greek. Or even in Portuguese.

Fellows slurped broodingly at his coffee. Pericles went back to packing liquor bottles in the crate. At length Fellows said, "We c'n git up a bigger posse than Barstow."

Pericles froze, half bent over the crate, his shoulders hunched up and his head back as if his nape had been touched by a hot iron. He waited.

"Scoop up our own records, huh?" muttered Fellows inevitably. "Hell, we c'n shoot our way through those shacks of his'n and be gone with th' papers before they know what's up. And it'll take a damn sight more'n twenty armed men an' a coupla court orders to pry us loose, this time."

"Now, Fellows," said Pericles carefully. "Don' talk this

kind stuff, you hear? You get troops from Topeka an' a rope for your neck."

"Not me," snarled the youngster. "I'll get lead in my blood, or I'll be over th' border afore that happens."

"Fellows," said Pericles pleadingly, "you can't fight everyt'ing with guns. Yes? Sometimes you got to use somet'ing else."

"Fer the likes o' Barstow? What *you* goin' to do? Use a skillet an' a han'ful o' cayenne? Maybe you want to feed Barstow an' his gunmen ontil they bust, huh?" He regarded the Greek with scorn, which changed to interest as he noticed what Pericles was doing. "What's the idea o' stashing all the firewater?"

"So it not break."

"Break how? You expectin' trouble here?" He leaped to his feet. "Someone pushin' you around, Peri? Who is it? Le's stop it afore it starts. Who do you want hawg-tied an' branded?"

"Shh, boy." Pericles almost laughed. "Don' you worry your head." He took down a hammer and battened the top of the crate. When he had finished he stood up, mopped his face and head, and came around the counter.

"Fellows, listen. You good feller, see? I don' wan' see you in bad trouble. Wait awhile, hun? Don' make this posse stuff. *Please*, Fellows, hun? This Meest' Barstow, he is a hard man. Well City got plenty guards, boy. Rifles. All night, until four o'clock in morning, it gets light a little, Barstow got guards out. You get posse, you get killed. Somebody get killed, anyway. Tamarisk men they get killed. Wait awhile, hun?"

"Wait, hell. Armed guards? This toad wants a war, does he? This one askin' fer it." Fellows scowled; then his head snapped up. "You say he pulls his guards an hour before sunup?"

"Sure. No need them. Men stirrin' about then anyway. But make to forget it, hun, Fellows? You a good boy. Don' get in bad trouble. Don' use you hosses for to make posse."

Having planted his seeds, Pericles bent to the task of sliding the heavy crate around behind the partition. That, oddly enough, placed it by the side door and its loading-stage, against which was backed his battered old buckboard.

Trask, the yard-goods merchant, an ex-sailor and a crack shot, reined in beside the glowering Fellows. Around them jogged the rest of the Tamarisk posse. A crescent moon showed the Well City trail vaguely, and pointed up the twin ruts of a wagon that had passed earlier.

"Hell of a note," grunted Trask. "Skedaddlin' around this time o' night. I tried to turn in after the meetin' an' didn't know whether I should stay up late or git up early. Turned in an' tried to sleep, still couldn't make up my mind, an' now" —he yawned hugely—"I don't rightly know if I'm awake or not. Way I feel, I wouldn't know silk f'm sailcloth."

"You damn well better be awake when we ride into Well City," said Fellows.

"Now, look, puppy," said the grizzled Trask. "Maybe you set this here forest fire, but just because we think you was right don't say you kin snap an' snarl at yer betters."

"Ah, it's that lousy Zapappas," said Fellows. "All this time claimin' he's a friend o' mine, an' then pullin' a thing like this," and he nodded at the wagon tracks. "What was it you tol' me about rats leavin' a founderin' ship?"

"Don't blame him too much," said Trask. "He's stuck with Tamarisk longer'n any of us an' he rates a break from it.

You know what they say about little fat guys. They're all good-natured because they can't fight an' they can't run."

"Thet's all right s'far as it goes," said Fellows. "But he didn't have to tote all thet likker over to Well City to grease his way into their gold mine."

Trask gave a reluctant, affirmative snort. "That was sorta small."

They went through the draw and emerged on a shelf overlooking Well City. There were two guttering fires to be seen north and south of the town, which was dark and still under the bright stars and the weak moonlight. The posse milled together and drew up.

"What time is it?"

"Not four yet."

Whup—whup—whoo-oop!

"Whut'n blazes was that?"

"A drunken poke if ever I heerd one."

There was a blaze of light in the largest building as the door was flung open, apparently blown by a gust of loose laughter.

"Ev'vy man Jack in th' town must be in there gettin' fried," somebody said.

"Yeah, on Zapappas's likker, the skonk," said another.

"Thet's one feller we'll squar' with, whatever."

"I brung a rope."

Somebody cracked a bullwhip. "This is better."

Trask spoke up. "It won't get Tamarisk a thing to stampede that little coyote. Let'm alone. He don't know what he's doin'."

"Feelin' real friendly, ain'tcha?" said an anonymous voice from the rear ranks. "Why don't you go on down and have a drink o' whisky?"

"Stow that," barked Trask. "We git to pullin' an' haulin' amongst ourselves, we won't get no town records out o' Well City. Now settle down fer about forty minutes. Mickey, get that there phony seizure paper of yours ready to whip out. You sure it's got enough 'whereas's' on it to keep 'em puzzled ontil we get clear with th' records?"

"That it has," said Mickey Mack. "*And* a gold seal. With ribbons."

"Good. Relax, boys. Talk quiet an' try to keep your hosses offen the rocks."

The posse dismounted and hobbled their mounts. Fellows lounged over to the Well City side of the draw and stood looking out at the half dozen shacks that were the county seat. A few feet down the slope from him were the shadowy masses of a large boulder and a small one. He felt the scalp muscles behind his ears contract at the faint hiss that suddenly reached him from the rocks. He froze, stared. Nothing. As he relaxed, the hiss was repeated.

Now, any other man there would have reported the matter and gotten cover for an investigation. But Fellows's approach was always a direct one. He tiptoed forward, gained the small boulder, waited tensely, then moved on to the larger one. Bracing himself with his hands, he peered carefully around it. Behind him, and between the two boulders, an extension of the black shadow reached out and lifted his gun from his holster, to jam it firmly into his spinal column, just below the shoulder blades.

"Walk," said a faint whisper.

The bruise-making solidity of the gunsight in his back was completely convincing. Without a sound he walked downgrade, without attempting to turn around or to make a sound, and the gun shifted only enough to steer him. His captor kept him to the blackest shadows, and turned him into the mouth of a dry gulch that opened on the draw a hundred yards away. *He won't shoot me if I don't make him,* he thought desperately. *The posse—*

The gun turned him to the wall. He stopped, his hands up. This was it, whatever "it" might be. "Well?" he said softly.

"Hey, boy. Don' be mad, hey."

"*Zapappas!*"

The gun muzzle rammed in agonizingly. "You be quiet with you mouth."

There was a tense silence, and then Fellows, breathing hard, whispered, "All right, Peri. You talk. I'll listen."

"At's good, boy," said Pericles in a low voice. "Hey, you t'ink they goin' hang me?"

"Reckon they will, Peri."

"Oh no. No. This wrong. You tell 'em."

"Me? I'd help 'em ef you'd get that equalizer out'n my back."

Surprisingly, Pericles's voice was gentle, and the gun was removed as he said sadly, "Sit down, Fellows. Here. Tak you gun."

Fellows stayed, stunned, where he was, face to the rock wall, hands raised, until Pericles's hand on his shoulder turned him around. The little man, he could see dimly was extending the gun to him. "Sit down, Fellows."

Then he talked. He talked for seven minutes, and it was not a gunshot, but a shout of laughter that brought the posse tumbling down the draw. There was no attack at four o'clock.

The bar of morning sunlight had crept so gradually on to Barstow's sodden face that it had not awakened him. He lay unbeautifully on his back, his collar and belt open, his

Eastern clothes rumpled, and his chin higher than his nose.

When the sunlight was abruptly cut off, however, he twitched, turned his head from side to side, moaned, clasped his temples, and sat up. Keeping his eyes tight shut, he shifted his hands cautiously over them, and in the soothing shade, ventured to ease the lids up. A vast throbbing inside his big head nudged another moan through his dry lips. "What a shindig," he muttered, "for a county seat. Hate to think of the high-jinks when we get to be a state capital."

Then it was he realized that there was someone standing over him, blocking the sunlight. He looked up quickly, wincing from the effort.

"Git up, Barstow," said Trask. "You're done."

"What are you doing in my—"

"Move," said Trask, and in such a tone that Barstow, without a second thought nor another syllable of bluster, moved. Trask waited while he pulled on his boots, and then stood aside, nodding toward the door. Barstow's gun belt hung over a chair near the window. Trask stood between it and the door. The belt stayed where it was as Barstow walked out.

The Easterner stopped dead as soon as he could see in the light. There was a clump of silent men around the well, watching him.

"H-How—what—" goggled Barstow. He turned, bellowed, "Smith! Oviedo!"

"They took off at daybreak," said Trask quietly. "The rest of your boys are with us, only maybe a little bit madder."

"I don't—I won't—" Barstow began, turning back toward his shack. Trask spun him around, placed his boot in the small of Barstow's back, and shoved. Barstow staggered a few steps, went to his knees, scrambled up again, and went toward the well, purely because the men there seemed less menacing than Trask, who followed close behind.

"Wh-what are you going to do?"

"Jest show you something," said Trask grimly. "Show him, boys."

Rough hands propelled Barstow through the crowd to the well. Fellows caught him there, put a hard young hand to the nape of the flabby neck, and shoved Barstow's head over the coping. "What do you see, Barstow?"

Barstow squirmed. "Nothing."

"Speak up, Barstow."

"The well is dry," said Barstow hoarsely.

"Why, Barstow?"

"Those drunken ——s!" swore Barstow. "They forgot to fill the well!"

"Filled it every night, didn't they, Barstow?"

"They—I—" He looked around at the men, some grinning, some glowering. He gulped and nodded his head.

Fellows guffawed. "That's it, boys. This swamp-frawg had men a-haulin' water from the spring, every night, when the rest o' his crew was sleepin'. Figgered to make this place the county seat, get the railroad through here, an' then sell his holdings an' clear out, leavin' someone else to worry about a dry well an' a useless town."

Barstow put his hands up to his face miserably, and slumped against the well. "What are you—" He licked his lips. "What are you going to do?"

"With you?" said Trask. "Why, we talked it over some. At first most of the boys wanted to throw you into your hole in the ground and fill it in. But we figger we'll do better to tell you how we found out about this, and then turn you loose. We like to think of you rememberin' it."

"It was that little guy you were tryin' to buy into your county seat," grinned Fellows. "Pericles Zapappas, his name is. He got to figgering. He's been in this country a long time, longer'n any of us, an' he knew damn well that there ain't no water to be dug for hereabouts. So he took up your invite an' came over here to look at your well. He was so sure there was somethin' wrong with it that he loaded his mare with two cook pots full of some stuff he brewed. After he left you he circled back and headed for th' spring. He seen enough of a beaten track up there to make him think he was right. He dropped his pots into th' spring. They wuz covered with sheep parchment and th' stuff in 'em leaked through real slow and flavored up th' water jest fine." He laughed again.

Trask took over. "He loads up his buckboard with hard likker last night and comes over here to help you celebrate gettin' the county seat—*after* goadin' Fellows here to git up a posse to shoot you loose from the county seat records. So thanks to him, all your hands got drunked up. Once he has you all nice and wound up, he takes a drink of water from the well. It tastes just like he knowed it would—like the stuff he put in the spring. That clinches it. He leaves y'all to waller in his likker and goes up to the draw yonder to wait for us."

"We was goin' to hang him," said Fellows with awe in his voice.

"Tell'm what Zapappas put in the spring, Fellows," said Trask.

"Tamarisk," said Fellows solemnly. "He's a great hand with the spices, he is. Stripped the bark of tamarisk and biled it down. It's bitter as hell. He uses it in his stew."

"Let's go, boys," said Trask. "Zapappas is back in Tamarisk by now, fixin' up the damnedest celebration breakfast this country has seen yet."

"What about me?" asked Barstow.

"You could drop dead," said Fellows helpfully.

"Yer county water commission," said Trask, "seems to of stole your hosses. You should be glad. Gives you a chance to walk off some o' that blubber. They's a tradin'-post forty mile up the valley, and a fort thirty mile the other way."

The last they saw of Barstow was a deflated, dejected figure squatting on the sand by his dry well, in sole possession of a county seat—a ghost town.

Riding through the draw, Trask said thoughtfully to Fellows, "It's a wonderful thing how a man'll fight with his own tools. I seen many a sailor brain people with a fid, and I seen a seamstress run a hatpin into a drunk. Zapappas, he fights right out'n his kitchen."

"Yup," said Fellows. "Usin' only kitchen tools." And he swore to himself to keep his bare back out of sight until those ring-shaped bruises on it disappeared.

Scars

THEODORE STURGEON

There is a time when a thing in the mind is a heavy thing to carry, and then it must be put down. But such is its nature that it cannot be set on a rock or shouldered off on to the fork of a tree, like a heavy pack. There is only one thing shaped to receive it, and that is another human mind. There is only one time when it can be done, and that is in a shared solitude. It cannot be done when a man is alone, and no man aloof in a crowd ever does it.

Riding fence gives a man this special solitude until his throat is full of it. It will come maybe two or three weeks out, with the days full of heat and gnats and the thrum of wire under the stretcher, and the night full of stars and silence. Sometimes in those nights a chunk will fall in the fire, or a wolf will howl, and just then a man might realize that his partner is awake too, and that a thing in his mind is heavy. If it gets to be heavy enough, it is put down softly, like fine china, cushioned apart with thick strips of quiet.

That is why a wise foreman pairs his fence riders carefully. A man will tell things, sometimes, things grown into him like the calluses from his wire cutters, things as much a part of him, say, as a notched ear or bullet scars in his belly; and his hearer should be a man who will not mention

them after sunup—perhaps not until after his partner is dead
—perhaps never.

Kellet was a man who had calluses from wire cutters, and
a notched ear, and old bullet scars low down on his
belly. He's dead now. Powers never asked to hear about it.
Powers was a good fence man and a good partner. They
worked in silence, mostly, except for a grunt when a post-
hole was deep enough, or "Here," when one of them handed
over a tool. When they pitched for the night, there was no
saying "You get the wood" or "Make the coffee." One or the
other would just do it. Afterward they sat and smoked, and
sometimes they talked, and sometimes they did not, and
sometimes what they said was important to them and sometimes it was not.

Kellet told about the ear while he was cooking one evening. Squatting to windward of the fire, he rolled the long-
handled skillet deftly, found himself looking at it like a man
suddenly studying the design of a ring he has worn for
years.

"Was in a fight one time," he said.

Powers said, "Woman."

"Yup," said Kellet. "Got real sweet on a dressmaker in
Kelso when I was a bucko like you. Used to eat there. Made
good mulligan."

They were eating, some ten minutes later, when he continued. "Long comes this other feller, had grease on his hair.
He shore smelt purty."

"Mexican?"

"Easterner."

Powers's silence was contributory rather than receptive at
this point.

"She said to come right in. Spoons him out what should

be my seconds o' stew. Gets to gigglin' an' fussin' over him."
He paused and chewed, and when the nutritious obstacle
was out of the way, spat vehemently. "Reckon I cussed a
little. Couldn't help m'self. Nex' thing you know, he's
a-tellin' me what language not to use in front of a lady. We
went round and round together an' that ended quick. See
this ear?"

"Pulled a knife on you."

Kellet shook his big, seamed head. "Nup. She hit me a lick
with the skillet. Tuk out part o' my ear. After, it tuk me the
better part of an hour with tar soap to wash the last o' that
hair grease offen my knuckles."

One bullet made the holes in his stomach. Kellet told
Powers laconically while they were having a dip in a cold
stream one afternoon.

"Carried a leetle pot-belly in them days," said Kellet.
"Bullet went in one side and out t'other. I figgered fer a
while they might's well rack me, stick me, bleed me, an'
smoke me fer fall. But I made it. Shore lost that pot-belly
in th' gov'ment hospital, though. They wouldn't feed me
but custards an' like that. My plumbin' was all mixed up an'
cross-connected.

"Feller in th' next bed died one night. They used t' wake
us up 'fore daybreak with breakfast. He had prunes. I shore
wanted them prunes. When I see he don't need 'em I ate
'em. Figgered nobody had to know." He chuckled.

Later, when they were dressed and mounted and following the fence, he added, "They found th' prune stones in
m' bandages."

But it was at night that Kellet told the other thing, the
thing that grew on like a callus and went deeper than bullet
scars.

Powers had been talking, for a change. Women. "They always got a out," he complained. He put an elbow out of his sleeping bag and leaned on it. Affecting a gravelly soprano, he said, "I'd like you better, George, if you were a gentleman."

He pulled in the elbow and lay down with an eloquent thump. "I know whut a gentleman is. It's whatever in the world you cain't be, not if you sprouted wings and wore a hello. I never seen one. I mean, I never seen a man yet where some woman, some time, couldn' tell him to ack like he was one."

The fire burned bright, and after a while it burned low. "I'm one," said Kellet.

Powers then felt that thing, that heavy growth of memory. He said nothing. He was awake, and he knew that somehow Kellet knew it.

Kellet said, "Know the Pushmataha country? Nuh—you wouldn't. Crick up there called Kiamichi. Quit a outfit up Winding Stair way and was driftin'. Come up over this little rise and was well down t'ord th' crick when I see somethin' flash in the water. It's a woman in there. I pulled up pronto. I was that startled. She was mothernekkid.

"Up she goes on t'other side 'til she's about knee-deep, an' shakes back her hair, and then she sees me. Makes a dive fer th' bank, slips, I reckon. Anyway, down she goes an' lays still.

"I tell you man, I felt real bad. I don't like to cause a lady no upset. I'd as soon wheeled back an' fergot the whole thing. But what was I goin' to do—let her drown? Mebbe she was hurt.

"I hightailed right down there. Figgered she druther be alive an' embarrassed than at peace an' dead.

"She was hurt all right. Hit her head. Was a homestead downstream a hundred yards. Picked her up—she didn' weigh no more'n a buffalo calf—an' toted her down there. Yipped, but there wasn't no one around. Went in, found a bed, an' put her on it. Left her, whistled up my cayuse, an' got to my saddlebags. When I got back she was bleedin' pretty bad. Found a towel fer under her head. Washed the cut with whisky. Four-five inches long under the edge of her hair. She had that hair that's black, but blue when the sun's on it."

He was quiet for a long time. Powers found his pipe, filled it, rose, got a coal from the dying fire, lit up, and went back to his bedroll. He said nothing.

When he was ready, Kellet said, "She was alive, but out cold. I didn't know what the hell to do. The bleedin' stopped for a while, but I didn't know whether to rub her wrists or stand on m' head. I ain't no doctor. Finally I just set there near her to wait. Mebbe she'd wake up, mebbe somebuddy'd come. Mebbe I'd have my poke full o' trouble if somebuddy did come—I knowed that. But what was I goin' to do —ride off?

"When it got dark two-three hours later I got up an' lit a tallow-fat lamp an' made some coffee. Used my own Arbuckle. 'Bout got it brewed, heard a funny kind of squeak from t'other room. She's settin' bolt-upright lookin' at me through th' door, clutchin' the blanket to her so hard she like to push it through to t'other side, an' makin' her eyes round's a hitchin'-ring. Went to her an' she squeaked ag'in an' scrambled away off into the corner an' tole me not to touch her.

"Said, 'I won't, ma'am. Yo're hurt. You better take it easy.'

"'Who are you?' she says. 'What you doin' here?' she says.

"I tol' her my name, says, 'Look, now, yo're bleedin' ag'in. Just you lie down, now, an' let me fix it.'

"I don't know as she trusted me or she got faint. Anyway down she went, an' I put a cold cloth on the cut. She says, 'What happened?'

"Tole her, best I could. Up she comes ag'in. 'I was bathin'!' she says. 'I didn't have no—' and she don't get no further'n that, but squeaks some more.

"I says, straight out, 'Ma'am, you fell an' hurt yore head. I don't recall a thing but that. I couldn't do nought but what I did. Reckon it was sort of my fault. I don't mean you no harm. Soon's you git some help I c'n leave. Ain't you got no menfolks?'

"That quieted her down. She tole me about herself. She was homesteadin'. Had pre-emption rights an' eighteen months left t'finish th' term. Husband killed in a rockslide. Swore to him she'd hold th' land. Didn't know what she'd do after, but spang shore she was a-goin' to do that first. Lot o' spunk."

Kellet was quiet again. The loom of the moon took black from the sky and gave it to the eastward ridge. Powers's pipe gurgled suddenly.

"Neighbor fourteen mile downstream was burned out the winter before. Feller eight mile t'other way gone up to Winding Stair for a round-up, taken his wife. Be gone another two months, mebbe. This little gal sweat out corn and peas fer dryin', had 'tater put by. Nobuddy ever come near, almost. Hot day, she just naturally bathed in th' crick.

"Asked her what about drifters like me, but mebbe gunmen. She reached under th' bed, drug out a derringer. Says,

'This's for sech trash.' An' a leetle pointy knife. 'This's for me,' she says, just like that. I tol' her to keep both of 'em by her. Was that sorry for her, liked her grit so, I felt half sick with it.

"Was goin' to turn in outside, by the shed. After we talked some an' I made her up some johnny-cake, she said I c'd bunk in th' kitchen if I wanted. Tol' her to lock her door. She locked it. Big wooden bar. I put down m' roll an' turned in."

The moon was a bead on the hill's haloed brow; a coronet, then a crown.

Powers put his pipe away.

"In th' mornin'," said Kellet, "she couldn't get up. I just naturally kicked th' door down when she didn't answer. Had a bad fever. Fast asleep an' wouldn't wake up but for a half minute, then she'd slide off ag'in. Set by her 'most all day, 'cept where I saw to my hoss an' fixed some vittles. Did for her like you would for a kid. Kept washin' her face with cold water. Never done nothin' like that before; didn't know much what to do, done the best I could.

"Afternoon, she talked for a hour or so, real wild. Mostly to her man, like he was settin' there 'stead o' me. He was a lucky feller. Be damned to you what she said—but I tuk to answerin' her once in a while, just 'Yes, honey,' when she got to callin' hard for him. Man a full year dead, I don't think she really believed it, not all the way down. She said things to him like—like no woman ever thought to say to me. He was a lucky feller. Be *damned* to you what she said. Anyhow, when I answered thataway she'd talk quiet. If I didn't she'd jest call and call, an' git all roiled up, an' her head would bleed.

"Next day she was better, but weak's a starvelin' colt in

a blowin' drought. Slept a lot. I found out where she'd been jerkin' venison, an' finished it up. Got some weeds outen her blackeye peas. Went back ever' now an' then to see she was all right. Remembered some red haw back over the ridge, rode over there and gathered some, fixed 'em to sun so's she'd have 'em fer dried-apple pie come winter.

"Four-five days went by like that. Got a deer one day, skinned it an' jerked it. Done some carpenterin' in th' shed an' th' house. Done what I could. Time I was fixin' the door to the kitchen I'd kicked down that first mornin', she lay a-watchin' me an' when I was done, she said I was good. 'Yo're good, Kellet,' she says. Don't sound like much to tell it. Was a whole lot."

Powers watched the moon rise and balance itself on the ridge, ready to float free. A single dead tree on the summit stood against it like a black-gloved hand held to a golden face.

Kellet said, "Just looka that ol' tree. So strong-lookin', an' so dead—"

When the moon was adrift, Kellet said, "Fixed that door with a new beam and good gudgeons. Man go to kick it down now'd have a job to do. She—"

Powers waited.

"—she never did use it. After she got well enough to get up an' around a bit, even. Just left it open. Mebbe she never thought about it. Mebbe she did too. Nights, I'd stretch out in my bedroll, lay there, an' wait. Pret' soon she'd call out, 'Good night, Kellet. Sleep good, now.' Thing like that, that's worth a passel o' farmin' and carpenterin'—

"One night, ten-eleven days after I got there, woke up. She was cryin' there in th' dark in t'other room. I called out what's the matter. She didn't say. Just kept a-bawlin'. Figgered mebbe her head hurt her. Got up, went to th' door. Asked her if she's all right. She just keeps a-cryin'-not loud, mind, but cryin' hard. Thing like that makes a man feel all tore up.

"Went on in. Called her name. She patted the side o' the bed. I set down. Put my hand on her face to see if she was gettin' a fever ag'in. Face was cool. Wet, too. She tuk my hand in her two an' held it hard up ag'in her mouth. I didn't know she was so strong.

"Set there quiet for two-three minutes. Got m' hand loose. Says, 'What you bawlin' for, ma'am?'

"She says, 'It's good to have you here.'

"I stood up, says, 'You git back to yore rest now, ma'am.' Went back to my bed. She—

"—cried mebbe a hour. Stopped sudden, an' altogether. Mebbe I slept after that, mebbe I didn't. Don't rightly recall.

"Next mornin' she's up bright an' early, fixin' chow. First time she's done it since she's hurt. Tole her, 'Whoa. Take it easy, ma'am. You don't want to tucker yorself out.'

"She says, 'I could of done this three days ago.' Sounded mad. Don't rightly know which one of us she's mad at. Fixed a powerful good breakfast.

"That day seemed the same, but it was 'way differ'nt. Other days we mostly didn't talk nothin' but business—caterpillars in th' tomato vines, fix a hole in th' smoke shed, an' like that. This day we talked the same things. Difference was, we had t' try hard to keep the talk where it was. An' one more thing—didn't neither of us say one word 'bout any work that might have to get done—tomorrow.

"Midday, I gathered up what was mine, an' packed my saddlebags. Brought my hoss up to th' shed an' watered him an' saddled him. She didn't say nothin'. Didn't see her much, but knowed she's watchin' me from inside th' house.

"All done, went to pat my hoss once on th' neck. Hit him so hard he shied. Right surprised m'self.

"She come out then. She stood a-lookin' at me. Says, 'Good-by, Kellet. God bless you.'

"Says good-by to her. Then didn't neither of us move for a minute. She says, 'You think I'm a bad woman.'

"Says, 'No sech a damn thing, ma'am! You was a sick one, an' powerful lonesome. Yo're all right now.'

"She says, 'I'm all right. I'll be all right long as I live,' she says, 'thanks to you, Kellet. Kellet,' she says, 'you had to think for both of us, an' you did. Yo're a gentleman, Kellet,' she says.

"Mounted, then, an' rode off. On the rise, looked back, saw her still by the shed, lookin' after me. I waved m' hat. She didn't move. Rode on."

The night was a white night now, since the moon had shucked its buoyant gold for its traveling silver. Powers heard Kellet turn over, and knew he could speak now if he cared to. Somewhere a mouse screamed briefly under an owl's silent talons. Distantly a coyote's hungry call built itself into the echoing loneliness.

Powers said, "So that's whut a gentleman is. A man thet c'n think fer two people when the time comes fer it?"

"Naw," drawled Kellet scornfully. "That's just what she come to believe because I never touched her."

Powers asked it, straight. "Why didn't you?"

A man will tell things, sometimes, things grown into him like the calluses from his wire cutters, things as much a part of him as, say, a notched ear or bullet scars in his belly; and his hearer should be a man who will not mention them after sunup—perhaps not until after his partner is dead—perhaps never.

Kellet said, "I cain't."

Cactus Dance

THEODORE STURGEON

The book, they decided, would bring Fortley Grantham back East if nothing else would, and at first I'd agreed with them. Later, I didn't know. Later still, I hardly cared, for it grew heavy in my pack. Once, somewhere in the desert between Picacho and Vekol, two prospectors found me squatted on the scorching sand, heat-mad, dreaming out loud. It wouldn't do for them to explain to me about the puncture in my canteen; I insisted that the book had soaked up my water as I walked, and I could get it back by wringing it out. I still have the book, and on it still are my teethmarks.

By train and stage and horse and mule I went, and, when I had to, on foot. I cursed the Territories in general and Arizona in particular. I cursed Prescott and Phoenix and Maricopa; Sacaton on the Gila River Reservation and Snowflake on Silver Creek. At Brownell in the Quijotas I learned that William Howard Taft had signed the enabling act that would make a state of that hellish country, and thereafter I cursed him too. From time to time I even cursed myself and the stubborn streak which ran counter to comfort and career and intelligence itself—it would have been so simple, so wise, to go back to the green lawns of the Institute, the tinkle of teacups, to soft polite laughter and the coolness of ivied libraries.

But most of all—from his books to his beard, from his scalp to his scholarship—I cursed Fortley Grantham, who had leaped from the envied position of the Pudley Chair in Botany into this dehydrated wilderness. He could have died under the wheels of a brewery-dray, and I'd have wept and honored him. He might have risen to be Dean, perhaps even to Chairman. Failing these things, if he felt he must immolate himself in this special pocket of Hell, why could he not resign?

But no, not Fortley Grantham. He simply stayed out West, drifting, faintly radiating rumors that he was alive. If mail ever reached him, he never answered it. If he intended to return, he informed no one. He would not come back, he would not be decently dead, he would not resign.

And I wanted that Chair! I had worked for it. I had earned it. What was I to do—wait for some sort of Enoch Arden divorce between Grantham and the Chair, so that he would be legally dead and the Chair legally vacant? No, I must find him or his grave, bring him back or prove him dead.

His last letter had come from Silver King, and at Silver King they told me he'd gone to Florence. He had not, and I was tired and sick when I got there to learn that. A Mohave up from Arizona had seen him, though, and from there the trail led along the Union Pacific to Red Rock and then to the railhead at Silverbell.

Had it not been for a man of the cloth at Silverbell, a Reverend Sightly, I'd have lost the trail altogether. But the good man told me with horror in his voice, of the orgies indulged in by the local Indians, who sat in a ring around a fire gobbling mescal buttons and having visions. I took the trouble to correct the fellow as to the source of the narcotic, which comes from the peyotl and not from the mescal at all, whereupon he grew positively angry with me—not, as I first supposed, because I had found him in error, but because he took me to be "that unholy scoundrel who has brought the gifts of science to aid and abet the ignorant savage in his degraded viciousness."

When at last I convinced the reverend of the innocence of my presence and person, he apologized and explained to me that a renegade botanist was loose in the desert, finding the rare and fabled peyotl with unheard-of accuracy, and trading the beastly stuff to whoever wanted it.

From that point on the trail was long and winding, but at least it was clear. When I could, I inquired after Grantham, and when no one had heard of Grantham I had merely to ask about the problem of obtaining mescal buttons. Always there were stories of the white man who was not a prospector nor a miner nor a drummer nor anything else but the purveyor of peyotl. He was a tall, broad man with a red-and-silver beard and a way of cocking his head to one side a bit when he spoke. That was Grantham, all right—may the vultures gulp his eyeballs and die of it . . .

Between the Eagle Tails and Castle Dome is the head of Posas Valley, and at its head is a filthy little oasis called Kofa. I confess I was happy to see it. It was August, and the heat and the glare had put knobs like knuckles in my sinus tissues; I could feel them grind together as I breathed.

I was afoot, the spavined nag I had bought in Arlington having died in New Water Pass. I had a burro for my pack and gear, and it was all she could handle. She was old and purblind, and if she had left her strength and durability behind with her youth, she had at least left her stubbornness too. She carried the little she could and let me walk.

I could hardly have been more depressed. I had little money left, and less hope. My canteen was a quarter-full of tepid mud which smelled faintly of the dead horned toad I'd seen in the waterhole in the pass. My feet hurt and my hipjoints creaked audibly as I plodded along. Half silently I mumbled what I once facetiously had called my "Anthem for Grantham," a sort of chant which ran:

. . . *I shall people his classroom with morons. I shall have him seduced by his chambermaid and I shall report it to the Dean. I shall publicly refute his contention that the* Echinopsis *cacti are separate from the genus* Cereus. *I shall lock him in his rooms at banquet time on Founder's Day. I shall uproot his windowboxes and spread rumors about him with the Alumni Association . . .*

It was the only way I had left of cheering myself up.

For weeks I had trailed the rumors of Grantham's peyotl traffic farther and farther from peyotl grounds. It was sahuro country here, and all about they stretched their yearning, other-worldly arms out and upward, as if in search for a lover who might forget their thorns. Down the valley, westward, was a veritable forest of Dracenoideae, called yucca hereabouts. I did not know if yucca and peyotl could coexist, and I thought not. If not, my main method of trailing Grantham was lost.

In such hopeless depression I staggered into Kofa, which, primitive as it was, afforded a chance of better company than my black thoughts and a doddering burro. I knew better than to hope for a restaurant and so went to the sole source of refreshment, the bar.

It seemed so dark inside, after the merciless radiance outside, that I stood blinking like an owl for thirty seconds before I could orient myself. At last I could locate the bar and deduce that a man stood behind it.

I croaked out an order for a glass of milk, which the bartender greeted with a thundering laugh and the quotation of a price so fantastic that I was forced to order whiskey, which I despise. The fool's nostrils spread when I demanded water with the whiskey, but he said nothing as he poured it from a stone jar.

I took the two glasses as far back in that 'dobe cavern as I could get from him, and slumped down into a chair. For a long moment there was nothing in my universe but the feel of my lips in the water, which, though alkaline, was wet and cool.

Only then, leaning back and breathing deeply, did I realize that someone sat across the table from me. He cocked his head on one side and said, "Well, well! If Mahomet won't come to the mountain, the Institute brings forth a mouse."

"Dr. Grantham!"

He watched me for a moment and then laughed. It was the same laugh, the deep rumble, the flash of strong white teeth which I used to envy so much. His eyes opened after it and he leaned forward. "Better shut your mouth now, sonny."

I had not realized it was open. I shut it and felt it with my fingers while I looked at him. He was in worn Levi's and a faded shirt to which had been sewn four or five extra pockets and a sort of shoulder cape with its lower edge cut into a fringe in the buckskin style. His hair and beard were untrimmed. His hands seemed stiff with yellowish calluses in the palms, and they were indifferently clean. A broad strap hung over one shoulder and across his chest to support

a large leather pouch. He was a far cry from Fortley
Grantham, M.A., F.B.S., D. Sc., with lifetime tenure of the
Pudley Chair in Botany at the Institute; yet there was no
mistaking him.

"Big Horn!" he roared to the bartender. "Set 'em up here.
This here's a perfessor from back East an' we're goin' to have
a faculty meetin'." That's how he pronounced it—"perfessor." He dealt me a stunning thump on the left biceps.
"Right, Chip?"

"Chip?" I looked behind me; there was no one there. And
the bartender's name obviously was Big Horn. It penetrated
that he was calling me Chip. "You surely haven't forgotten
my name, Doctor."

"I surely ain't, Doctor," he said mimicking my voice. He
smiled engagingly. "Everybody's got two names," he explained, "the name they's born with an' the name I think
they ought to have. The name you ought to have, now, it's
Chip. There's a little crittur lives in an' out of the rocks,
sits up straight an' looks surprised, holds up its two little
paws, an' lets its front teeth hang out. Chipmunk, they call it
back East, though it's a rock squirrel other places. Get me,
Chip?"

I put both hands on the table and pressed my lips together. Big Horn arrived just then and put more whiskey
down before me. I said coldly, "No, thank you." Big Horn
paid absolutely no attention to me, but walked away leaving the whiskey where it was.

"Come on, climb down. This ain't the hallowed halls."

"That is the one thing I'm sure of," I said haughtily.

He shook his head in pity. He looked down at his glass
and his eyebrows twitched. He made no attempt to say anything and I began to feel that perhaps I, not he, should be

making the overtures. I said, for want of anything better, "I suppose 'Big Horn' is another of your appellations."

He nodded. "To him it's sort of compliment." He laughed. "Some people carry their vanity in the damnedest places."

I felt I should not pursue this, somehow. He tilted his head and said, "You're not jumpin' salty because I call you Chip?"

"I don't read a compliment into it."

"Shucks, now, son—they're real purty little animals!" He waved. "Drink up now, an' warm yoreself. I'm not insultin' you. You wouldn't be wonderin' about it if I did—I'd see to that. Don't you understand, I was callin' you Chip—privately, I mean—from the minute I saw you, years back."

"I was beginning to think," I said acidly, "that you had forgotten everything that happened before you came to Arizona."

"Never fear, colleague," he intoned, in precisely the voice that once boomed through the lecture halls. "I can still distinguish a rhizome from a tuber and a faculty tea from deep hypnosis." Instantly he reverted to this appalling new self. "I got a handle too. They call me Buttons."

"To what characteristic is that attributed?"

He looked at me admiringly. "I druther listen to that kind of talk than a thirsty muleskinner cussin'." He pulled at the thongs that tied down the flap of his pouch, reached in, and tossed a handful of what seemed to be small desiccated mushrooms to me.

I picked one up, squeezed it, turned it over, smelled it. "Lophophora."

"Good boy," he said sincerely. "Know which one?"

"Williamsii, I think."

"Sharp as a sidewinder's front fang," he said, giving me

another of those buffets. "Hereabouts they're mescal buttons."

"Oh," I said. "Oh yes. So they call you Buttons. You—
uh—are rather widely known in connection with this—uh—
vegetable."

He laughed. "I didn't think a botanist ever used the word
'vegetable.'"

I ignored this. I rose. "One moment, please, I think I can
show you that you have a wider reputation in this matter
than you realize."

He made as if to stop me but did not. I went out to my
burro. She was standing like a stone statue in the blazing
sun, her upper lip just touching the surface of the water in
the horse-trough, breathing water-vapor in patient ecstasy. I
dug into my pack and wormed out the book. Inside again, I
placed it carefully by Grantham's glass.

He looked at it, at me, then picked it up. Holding it high,
he moved his head back and his chin in with the gesture of a
seaman forcing his horizoned eyes to help with threading a
needle.

"Journal of the Botanical Sciences," he read. "Catalogue,
Volume Four, revised. 1910, huh? Right up to the minute.
Oh bully." He squinted. "Cactaceae. Phyla and genera reclassified. Hey, Big Horn," he roared, "the perfessor here's
got reclassified genera."

The bartender clucked sympathetically. Grantham leafed
rapidly. "Nice. Nice."

"We thought you'd like it. Look up lophophora."

He did. Suddenly he grunted as if I had kneed him, and
stabbed a horny forefinger onto the page. "'Lophophora
granthamii' I'll be Billy-be-damned! So they took note of old
Grantham, did they?"

"They did. As I said, you are widely known in connection with peyotl."

He chuckled. He made no attempt to hide the fact that he was vastly pleased.

"When you were sending back specimens and reports, you were of great value to us," I pointed out. I coughed. "Something seems—ah—to have happened."

He kept his eyes on the listing, wagging his big head delightedly. "Yup, yup," he said. "Something happened." He suddenly snapped the book closed and slid it across to me. "Last thing in the world I ever expected to see again."

"I didn't think you would, either," I said bitterly. "Dr. Grantham—"

"Buttons," he corrected.

"Dr. Grantham, I have traveled across this continent and through some of the most Godforsaken topography on earth just to put this volume in your hands."

He started. I think that he realized only then that I had sought him out, that this was no accident on a field trip.

"You didn't!" He lifted his glass and tossed it to his lips, found it empty, looked around in a brief confusion, then reached and took mine. He wiped his mouth with the bristly back of his hand. "What in hell for?"

I tapped the book. "If I may speak frankly—"

"Fire away."

"We felt that this might—uh—bring you back to your senses."

"I got real healthy senses."

"Dr. Grantham, you don't understand. You—you—" I floundered, picked up my second whiskey and drank some of it. It made my eyes stream. My throat made a sort of death-rattle and suddenly I could breathe again. I could feel the whiskey sinking a tap-root down my esophagus while tendrils raced up and out to my earlobes where, budding, they began to heat.

"You left for a field trip and did not return. You were granted your sabbatical year to cover this because of your prominence in the field and because of the excellence of the collections you sent back; specimens such as the peyotl now named for you. Then the specimens dwindled and ceased, the reports dwindled and ceased—and then nothing, nothing at all."

He scratched his thick pelt of red-and-silver. "Reckon I just figured it didn't matter much no more."

"Didn't matter?" I realized I squeaked, and then that my voice was high and nagging, but I no longer cared. "Don't you realize that as long as you are alive you hold the Pudley Chair?"

I saw the glint in his eyes and clutched his wrist. "If you shout out to that bartender that you have a Pudley Chair, I'll—I'll—" I whispered, but could not finish for the cannonade of rich laughter he sent up. I sat tense and furious, helpless to do or say anything until he finished. At last he wiped his eyes.

"I'm sorry," he said sincerely, quite as if he were civilized. "You caught me off guard. I'm really sorry, Professor."

"It's all right," I lied. "Doctor, I want that Chair if you don't. I've worked hard for it. I've earned it. I—I need it."

"Well gosh, son, go to it. It's all yours."

I had wanted to hear that for so long. I'd dreamed of it so much—and now, hearing it, I became furiously angry. "Why didn't you resign?" I shouted. "That's all you had to do, resign, put a two-cent stamp on an envelope, save me all this work, this worry—I nearly died with a hole in my canteen," I wept, waving at the pottery kiln they call "outdoors" in this terrible land. "Two horses I killed—my work is waiting—my books, students—"

I found myself patting the table, inarticulate, glaring into his astonished eyes. "Why?" I yelled. "Why, why, why—" I moaned.

He got up and came round the table and stood behind me. On my shoulders he put two huge warm hands like epaulets. "I didn't know, son. I—damn it, I did know, I guess." I hated myself for it, but my shoulders shook suddenly. He squeezed them. "I did know. I reckon I just didn't care."

He took his hands away and went back to his chair. He must have made a sign because Big Horn came back with more whiskey.

After a time I said, with difficulty, "All the way out here I hated you, understand that? I'm not—I don't—I mean, I never hated anything before, I lived with books and people who talk quietly and—and scholastic honors . . . Damn it, Dr. Grantham, I admired and respected you, you understand? If you'd stayed at the Institute for the next fifty years, then for fifty years I'd've been happy with it. I admired the Chair and the man who was in it, things were the way they should be. Well, if you didn't want to stay, good: If you didn't want the Chair, good. But if you care so little about it—and I respect your judgment—you understand?

"Oh gosh yes. Shut up awhile. Drink some whiskey. You're going to bust yourself up again."

We sat quietly for a time. At length he said, "I didn't care. I admit it. Not for the Institute or the Chair nor you. I should've cared about you, or anyone else who wanted it as bad as you do. I'm sorry. I'm really sorry. I got—involved. Other things came to be important."

"Peyotl. Selling drugs to the Indians," I snarled. "You've probably got a nice little heap of gold dust salted away!"

The most extraordinary series of expressions chased each other across his face. I think if the first one—blind fury—had stayed, I'd have been dead in the next ten seconds.

"I don't have any money," he said gently. "Just enough for a stake every once in a while, so I can—" He stared out at the yellow-white glare. Then, as if he had not left an unfinished sentence, he murmured, "Peyotl! Professor, you know better than to equate these buttons with opium and hashish. Listen, right near here, in the seventeenth century, there used to be a mission called Santo de Jesús Peyotes. Sort of looks as if the Spanish priests thought pretty well of it, hm?

"Listen," he said urgently, "Uncle Sam brought suit against an Indian by the name of Nah-qua-tah-tuck, because Uncle's mails had been used to ship peyotl around. When the defense witnesses were through testifying about how peyotl-eaters quit drinking, went back to their wives, and began to work hard; when a sky pilot name of Prescott testified about his weekly services where he served the stuff to his parish, and they were the most Godfearing parish in the Territories, why, Uncle Sam just packed up and went right back home."

I knew something of the forensics of the alkaloid mescaline. I said, "Well and good, but you haven't told me how you—how you could—"

"Easy, ea—sy," he soothed, and just in time too. "Chip, you're the injured party, for sure. I wish I could—well, make up for it, part way."

"Perhaps we'd just better not talk about it."

"No, wait." He studied me. "Chip, I'm going to tell you about it. I'm going to tell you how a man like me could do what he's done, how he could find something more important than all the Institutes running. But—"

I waited.

"—I don't expect you to believe it. Want to hear it anyway? It's the truth."

I thought about it. If I left him now, the Chair waiting for me, my personal and academic futures assured—wouldn't that content me?

It wouldn't, I answered myself. Because Grantham wouldn't return or resign. I'd lost two years, almost. I should know why I'd lost them. I had to know. I'd lost them because Grantham was callous and didn't care; or because Grantham was crazy; or because of something much bigger "than all the Institutes running." Which?

"Tell me, then."

He hesitated, then rose. "I will." He thumped his chest, and it sounded like the grumble you hear sometimes after heat lightning. "But I'll tell it my way. Come on."

"Where?"

He tossed a thumb toward the west. "The forest."

The "forest" was the heavy growth of Draconaenoideae I'd seen down the valley. It was quite a haul and I was still tired, but I got up anyway. Grantham gave me an approving look. He went outside and unstrapped my pack from the burro. "We'll let Big Horn hold this." He took it inside and emerged a moment later.

"Why don't you leave your pouch?"

Grantham twinkled. "They call me Buttons, remember? I never leave this anywhere."

We walked for nearly an hour in silence. The yucca appeared along the trail in ones and twos, then in clusters and clumps with spaces between. Their presence seemed to affect Grantham in some way. He began to walk with his head up, instead of fixing his eyes on the path, and his mind God knows where.

"See there?" he said once. He pointed to what was left of a shack, weed-grown and ruined. I nodded but he had nothing more to offer.

A little later, as we passed a fine specimen of melocactus, the spiny "barrel," Grantham murmured, "It's easy to fall under the spell of the cacti. You know. It caught you a thousand miles away from here. Ever smell the cereus blooming at night, Chip? Ever wonder what makes the Turk's-head wear a fez? Why can't a chinch-bug make cochineal out of anything but nopal? And why the spines; why? When most of 'em would be safe from everyone and everything, even sliced up with gravy on . . ."

I answered none of the questions, because at first I thought them foolish. I thought, it's like asking why hair grows on a cat's back but not on its nose—then gradually I began to yield, partly because it seemed after all that a cactus is indeed a stranger thing than a cat—or a human, for that matter; and partly because it was Grantham, *the* Grantham, who murmured these things.

"This will do," he said suddenly, and stopped.

The trail had widened and then disappeared, to continue three hundred yards down the valley where again the yucca grew heavily. Flash floods had cut away the earth to leave an irregular sandy shelf on the north side, and Grantham swung up on this and squatted on his heels. I followed slowly and sat beside him.

He bowed his head and pressed his heavy eyebrow ridges against his knees, hugging his legs hard. He radiated tension, and just as noticeably, the tension went away. He raised his head slowly and looked off down the valley. I followed his gaze. The bald hills were touched to gold by the dropping sun, and their convoluted shadows were a purple that was black, or a black that was purple. Grantham began to talk.

"Back there. That shack."

He paused. I recalled it.

He said, "Used to be a family there. Mexican. Miguel, face as hard and bald as those hills, and a great fat wife like a suet pudding with a toupee. Inside Miguel was soft and useless and cruel the way only lazy people can be cruel. And the wife was hickory with thorns, inside, with another kind of cruelty. Miguel would never go out of his way to be kind. The woman would travel miles, work days on end, to be cruel.

"Kids."

Somewhere a lizard scuffled, somewhere a gopher sent the letter B in rapid, expert Morse. I held two fingers together, and with one eye closed used the fingers to cover the sun limb to limb. When the lower limb peeped under my finger, Grantham's breath hissed in and out quickly, once each, and he said, "They had kids. Two or three pigeon-breasted toddlers. One other. But I met her later.

"That was when I first came, when I was doing that collecting and reporting that impressed you all so much. I arranged with Miguel the same deal I had with others before: he was to keep his eyes open for this plant or that, or an unseasonal flower; and certain kinds he was to cut and save for me, and others he was to locate and lead me to. He'd get a

copper or two for what I liked, and once in a while a dime
just to keep 'em going. Quite a trick when no one speaks the
other's language and the signs you make mean different
things all around. Still, the law of averages figures here too,
and I always got my money's worth.

"I made my deal and he called in the family, all but one,
and when all the heads were nodding and the jabbering
stopped, I waved my hand and headed this way. Miguel
shouted something at me a moment later, and I turned and
saw them all clustered together looking at me bug-eyed, but
I didn't know what he meant, so I just waved and walked
on. They didn't wave back.

"I'd about reached where we're sitting now when I heard
a sort of growl up ahead. I'd been looking at the flora all the
way up, and never noticed the things I'd smell or hear or
just—just feel now. Anyway, I looked up and the first thing
I saw was a little girl standing here in the cut. The second
thing was a black roiling wall of water and cloud towering
up and over me, coming down like a dynamited wall. The
third thing was a gout of white spray thirty feet tall squirting
out of the landscape not a quarter of a mile away.

"How long does it take to figure things out at a time like
that? It was like standing still for forty minutes, thinking it
out laboriously, and at the same time being able to move
only two feet a minute like a slow loris. Actually I suppose
I looked up, then jumped, but a whole lot happened in that
second.

"I shouted and was beside the girl in two steps. She didn't
move. She was looking at the sky and the spume with the
largest, darkest eyes I have ever seen. She was a thin little
thing like the rest of Miguel's litter. She wasn't pretty; her
face was badly pocked and either she'd lost a front tooth

or so or the second set had never made up its mind to go on with the job.

"Thing is, she was a native and I wasn't. To me the flash flood was a danger, but she was completely unafraid. It wasn't a stupid calm. If ever there was a package of sensitivity, this was it. How can I describe it? Look, you know how a beloved house-cat watches you enter a room? The paws are turned under, the eyes are one-third open, and the purr goes on and on like a huge and sleepy bee. The cat can do that because it means no violence to you and you mean no violence to it.

"Now imagine coming suddenly on a wild deer—how would you feel if it looked up at you with just such fearlessness? It was as if violence couldn't occur near this girl. It was unthinkable. Before her was this hellish wall of water and beside her was a rather large bearded stranger shouting like a rag-peddler, and there she stood, awake, aware, not stunned, not afraid.

"I scooped her up and made for the bank. I—I had help. I thought at the time it was the vanguard of that tall press of wind. Later I thought—I don't know what I thought, but anyway, the yuccas folded toward me, tangling their leathery swords together; even at their tips I had something thick as your arm and strong as an anchor-cable to take hold of. I swung up past one, two, three of them that way and then the williwaw came down shouting and knocked me flat as a domino.

"I twisted as I fell so I wouldn't land on the child. I held her tight to me with my right arm, and I threw up my left as some sort of guard over both of us. I distinctly saw a forty-foot Chaya cactus twist past overhead, and then I was hit. By what, I couldn't say, but it hit my left forearm and my left fist came down on my chin, and that, for me, was the end of that part of the adventure.

"When I opened my eyes I thought first I'd gone blind, and then it came to me that it was night, a black, scudding night, cold the way only this crazy, either-or-and-all-the-way country can get. I was shaking like a gravel-sorter. Something had hold of my arm, which hurt, and I tried to pull it away and couldn't.

"It was the kid. She was crouched beside me, holding my left forearm in both her hands. She wasn't shivering. Her hands were warm, too, though I suppose anything over forty degrees would feel warm just then. I stopped pulling and heaved up to see what I could see. The scud parted and let a sick flicker of moon show through, and that helped.

"I had a five-inch gash in my arm—up and down, fortunately, not across, so it had missed any major blood-vessel. I could see the two ends of the cut, but between those ends lay the girl's hands. Their pressure was firm and unwavering, and clotted blood had cemented her to me nice as you please. And she'd been sitting there holding the edges of the cut together—how long? Three hours? Four, five? I didn't know. I don't know now.

"She tugged at me gently and we got our feet under us. We scrabbled down the bank until I could see the deep, strong creek that hadn't been there that afternoon. We went downstream a piece until the bank shelved, squatted by the edge, and got her hands and my arm together into the water. In a few moments she worked a hand free, then the other. I bled a bit then, but not too much, and she helped me tie on my kerchief.

"I sat down, partly to rest, mostly to look at her. She looked right back, with that same fearlessness showing even

in the scudding dark. I thanked her but she didn't say anything. I grinned at her but she didn't smile. She just looked
at me, not appraising, not defiant, just liking what she saw,
and unafraid.

"I took her back to Miguel's. The old lady was raising
particular hell, shaking her fists at the sky. Their rotten
corral-pole was down and they'd lost two head of their
hairy, bony, bot-ridden scrub cattle. I got a vague impression of two of the little ones staring big-eyed and scared
from the drafty corner. I propelled the girl forward to the
doorway and the old sow put out a claw and snatched her
inside. I thought she raised her fist but I wasn't ready to believe anything like that. Not that night. Then the door was
closed and I slogged off toward Kofa.

"About ten minutes later I saw her again, standing by the
bank just out of the shadows of the yucca. If the moon
hadn't flashed I'd have missed her altogether. She faded
back into the shadows and when I reached the place she was
gone, though I yelled my head off. I do believe she had
come to see for sure if I could navigate all right. How she
got clear of the house and passed me in the dark is another
thing I'll never know.

"It was a couple of days before I could get around easily
with that arm. It was badly bruised and it swelled like a
goatskin bottle, but the cut healed faster than a cut like that
ought to. Call it clean air and a good constitution, if you like.
Got any makings?"

"I don't smoke," I said.

"That's right." He sighed. "No matter.

"Well, a couple of days later I went back. Miguel had
quite a pile of stuff for me. Good stuff, too, a lot of it. A colchicum, or what looked like one, but without the bulging

'corm' at the base; a gloriosa with, by God, pink petals; a
Chaya only eight inches tall. Lot of junk, too, of course, and
maybe more treasures—I wouldn't know. I caught a movement out of the corner of my eye—and there just off
Miguel's reservation, the girl stood in the shadows.

"Herf!" he snorted, "once in the West Indies I cut into a
jungle glade and saw a wild magnolia as big as my head.
It was so big, so pale in the dimness that I was actually
scared; might just as well've been a lion for a second or so,
the way I jumped. This kid, she gleamed out of the
shadows the same way.

"Like the big brainless buffalo I am, I had to straighten up
and wave and grin, and before I could blink the old lady
flashed off and collared the kid. My God, you wouldn't believe how that two-ton carcass could move! She'd caught
her and had cuffed her in the face, forward and back, three
times before I could get the slack out of my jaw.

"I don't know what sort of a noise I made but whatever it
was it stopped her as if I'd thrown a brick. I got the girl away
from her and then I went back and with my machete I
chopped up the specimens into ensilage. Talk about sub-
stitution! I was wild!

"When the red fog went away I conveyed to Miguel that
there was no chapa for him this day nor any other day when
I saw them strike a child. Once he got the idea he turned
and bitterly berated his wife, who screamed some things
the gist of which was that I was an ungrateful scut because
she had hit the child only for bringing no specimens. Miguel
bellowed something to her and then turned to me all scrapes
and smiles, and promised to arrange everything any way I
wanted it.

"I growled like a grampus and charged off downstream.

I was mad at everything and everybody. I've since gotten a cormless colchicum but I never saw another dwarf Chaya. Well . . . the things you do . . .

"I'd stamped along perhaps a hundred yards before I became aware that I still held the girl's arm. I stopped at once and hunkered down and gave her a hug and told her how sorry I was.

"She had two angry welts on one side of her face and three on the other; and she had those eyes; and you know, those eyes were just the way they'd been when I first saw them, fearless and untouched and untouchable.

"I'd had a strange semi-dream the day before, when I was trying to sleep through the throbbing of my arm. It was a sort of visualization of what would have happened in the flood if I hadn't been there, like a cinematograph, if you've ever seen one of the things. There she stood, and when the water reached her it turned and went around her, and the wind too, just as if she were under a bell-jar. Hm! But it wasn't like that, and here were the bruises on her face to prove it. At the same time the vision was correct, for no matter what happened to her, it couldn't really reach her. See what I mean?"

"Cowed," I said. "Poor kid."

He put his hands together and squeezed them for a moment. I think he was angry at me. Then he relaxed. "Not cowed, Chip. You have to be afraid for that. Fearless, don't you understand? As much fear as a granite cliff looking at a hurricane, as much as a rose listening to garden shears."

"Beyond me," I said.

"Beyond me too," he said immediately. He looked at me. "I'll stop now?"

"Stop? No!"

"Very well. Don't forget, I didn't tell you to believe me. All I said was that it was the truth." He looked up at the sky. "I must hurry . . .

"She didn't answer my hug or my apologies, but somehow I knew they reached the places where fear could not. Then I remembered what was in my specimen bag. I'd managed to find a child's dress in the trading post at Kofa. It was white with blue polka dots all over it, made of some heavy, hard-finish material that ought to wear a hole in sandpaper. I didn't think too much of it myself—it was only the best I could do—but I can't describe what happened when I handed it over.

"I mean just that, Chip—I can't describe it. Look, she couldn't or wouldn't talk. Whether she could hear or not I don't know. And she might as well have been born without motor nerves in her face, or at least her cheeks, because not once did she ever smile.

"Yet she stood looking at the dress when I shook it out, and perhaps her eyes got rounder. She didn't move, so I held it up against her. She put those eyes on me and slowly brought her hands together in front of her. I nodded my head and smiled and told her go ahead, put it on, it's for you. And then she—"

Grantham twisted his thick forefinger into and out of his beard, picked up a pebble, threw it, watching studiously.

"—began to glow," he continued. "This Arizona moon, in the fall, when the brush-fires shroud the sky . . . the moon's up, full, off the hills and you can't see it, and gradually you know it's there. It isn't a thing, it's a place in the sky, that's all. Then it rises higher, and the smoke blows down, and it gets brighter and brighter and brighter until—you don't know how or just when—you realize you could read a man's palm by it. The kid did that, somehow. When whatever she felt was at peak you—sort—of—had to squinch up your eyes to see her." He punched the sand. "I don't know," he muttered.

"She put up her hands to shuck out of the rag she was wearing and I turned my back. In a second she danced past me, wearing the blue-dotted dress. Her and that quiet, pock-marked, unsmiling little face, glowing like that, spinning like a barn swallow, balancing like a gull. Ever see a bird smile, Chip? A lily laugh? Does a passion-flower have to sing? Hell. I mean, hell. Some people don't have to say anything.

"That was the first day I saw her do what I called her Yucca Dance. She stood on the cap of a rise in the yucca forest and the fresh damp buffalo grass hiding her feet. With her elbows close to her sides, her forearms stretched upward and her hands out, she just barely moved her fingers, and I suddenly got the idea—the still, thick stem, the branching of leaves, the long slender neck and crown of flowers.

"I laughed like a fool and ran to the nearest cactus. I pulled two firm white blossoms and went and put them in her hair, and stepped back, laughing. Both of them fell out, and she made no attempt to pick them up. I caught her eyes then, and I got the general idea that I'd made some sort of mistake. I stumbled back, feeling like a damn idiot, and she went back into her trance, being a yucca awaiting the wind.

"And when the wind came she made the only sound I ever heard from her, but for her footsteps. It was, in miniature, precisely the whispering of the leather leaves touching together. When the wind gusted, her whisper was with it, and she leaned with—with the—other—Chip?"

I said, "Yes, Grantham."

"You don't forget it, standing in her white dress with blue spots, rooted and spreading and stretched, whispering in the wind. Chip?"

I answered again.

"You know about the moth, Chip?"

I said, "Pronuba yuccasella."

He grinned. It was good to see his face relax. "Good entomology, for a botanist."

"Not especially," I said. "Pronuba's a fairly botanical sort of bug."

"Mmm." He nodded. "It doesn't eat anything but yucca nectar and the yucca blossom can be fertilized by no other insect. Chip, did you know a termite can't digest cellulose?"

"Out of my line."

"Well, it can't," said Grantham. "But there's a bacterium lives in his belly that can. And what he excretes, the termite feeds on."

"Symbiosis," I said.

"Wonder how you'd get along," he mused, "with folks who didn't know as much as you do? Yes, symbiosis. Two living things as dissimilar as a yucca and a moth, and neither can live without the other."

"Like Republicans and Dem—"

"Ah, stow it, cork it, and shove it," Grantham said bluntly. He looked at the western hills, and the light put blood on his great lion's head. "Pretty natural thing, that symbiosis. Lot of it around."

He began to talk again, rapidly, with, now and again, a quick glance at the darkling west. "Six months, seven, maybe, I collected around here. No trouble with Miguel. He collected a bunch of weeds and sticks, but once in a while he earned his keep, retroactively. The old lady kept

her hands off. The kid spent every day with me. I guess I
had the area pretty well sieved in four months, but I went
out every day anyhow."

"I remember," I said.

"Yes, yes, I didn't send so many specimens. Later, none.
I know. I said I was sor—"

For the first time I barked at him. "Go on with your
story."

"Where—oh. The moth. The moth that won't go near anything but a yucca."

I thought he had forgotten me. "Hey," I said.

"She danced," he said, examining his hands carefully in
the dim light, "any time it occurred to her, for a long time or
a little. Or at night. At night," he said clearly, heaving himself upright and not looking at me, "the petals open and the
moths fly. They were a cloud around her head."

I waited. He said, "It's only the truth. And once in the
late sunset, still some light, and me close to her, I saw a
moth crawl into her ear. I got scared, I—put out my hand to
do something, pluck it out, shake her, do something. She
raised her hand, slowly—or it seemed to be slowly, but it was
there before my hand was. She just stood, still as a tree,
waiting, and the moth came out again."

I didn't say anything. Not anything at all. We sat watching the western mountain.

"I went away," said Grantham, his words stark and clear
against the heat inside him. "To get more specimens, you
understand."

"Some more came," I said.

"I was away for three months. A long time. Too long.
Then I had no business back in Kofa but I went back any-

way—oh, in case I'd left anything there or something. I was supposed to go back to the Institute, I guess. Mm.

"The first face I saw in Kofa that I knew was Miguel's. I fell over him. He was standing like a brown statue on the duckboards near the saloon and I tripped and knocked his hat off. I pulled him to his feet and asked him *Com' esta?*

"*Malo, muy malo* and a flood of north-Mex is all I could get. I guess I looked a little foolish. Why is it when you talk to someone who doesn't know your language, you holler at him? Finally I got impatient and ran him into the bar. I asked Big Horn what Miguel was trying to tell me.

"The general idea was that the little ones had died. I never did find out how many, two or three. Miguel shrugged at this, took off his hat, raised his eyes and his eyebrows, in that order, at the ceiling. I gather he felt no responsibility over this; such matters were out of his hands, but one could always make more. What bothered Miguel, Big Horn told me, was the loss of his wife, who had broken her leg, gotten a bone infection, and died *muy rapido*. She had been, it seemed, a very hard worker.

"The girl? He didn't know. He didn't know any more after I got excited and tried to shake it out of him. Big Horn was over the bar with his bung-starter before I could pull myself together. He never minded anybody getting rough at his bar providing both parties were enjoying it. He pointed out to me that Miguel had come in here peaceably even if I hadn't. Then he sat Miguel down and questioned him quietly while I fumed, and then he told Miguel to go, which he did much faster than usual.

"'He says,' Big Horn told me, 'that the girl just wandered away. He says she always spent more nights out in the yucca forest than home anyhow. She went away and she just didn't come back. He says he went looking for her, too, after the old lady died. I guess he wanted his tortillas pounded. He looked real hard.'

"I told him thanks, and came out here. I wish you had the makings, Chip."

"Sorry," I said.

"I came out here and wandered for a while. A man can eat out here, sleep out here, right time of year. You could, Chip, knowing it just from books. I guess I felt real bad. Funny thing," he mused. "I wanted to call her, but I had never found out what her name was."

He was quiet. The evening breeze sprang and died, stopped and pressed and sprang again. The yuccas whispered and whispered.

"Hear?"

"I hear," I said.

"I heard it one night, sleeping here, and came up standing. There was no wind. She was here, right here, Chip. Dancing like a yucca, whispering."

"See her?"

"No, I didn't see her." I couldn't see his face, but I knew he was smiling, and I wondered what in time he was smiling about.

"You, Professor, you want something more than you want anything else there is, more than money or your name in books or a woman. You want the Pudley Chair in Botany. I bet you'd kill anyone who tried to get it away from you."

"Anyone but you."

His fringed shirt rustled as he twisted toward me. "You mean that. You do mean that. That's fine, Chip. That's nice." He rested his chin on his knees and paid attention to the evening star. "Everybody wants some one single thing that bad. Some get it, some don't. Some know what it is, some never find out. You found out. I found out."

"Want to tell me?"

"Sure I do. Sure. Chip, no offense, but you and I are different kinds of botanist."

"I know that. But—well, go on."

"You want botany out of books. Some window boxes, some lab, sure. You learned it right; there's not a thing wrong in being that way, you see? Very valuable. You learned botany so's you could be a botanist, the best damn botanist in the world, if you could make it. You might make it too."

"And you?"

"I got to be a botanist so I could be—close to something. Something like that symbiosis you were talking about. I'm a man, but man and cloverleaf, man and Chaya, man and piñon juniper—is that so much crazier than moth and cactus?"

"How close do you think you can carry this symbiosis of yours? Or was it just a figure of speech?"

"Time to show you, I reckon," he said. He rose. I followed. "It's dark."

"Sure," he said. "I know the way. Hook on to the back of my belt."

I did, and he strode off purposefully into the pitch-black shadows of the yucca. How we turned, climbed, slithered, I couldn't say. It might have been a long way, and it might have been a circle.

We stopped. He fumbled in his pouch. "It's her birthday."

"How do you know?" I whispered. This was a place to whisper.

"Just know. Pick a day, stay with it from then on. Amounts to the same thing. Here."

He put something into my hand. Cloth, very fine cloth. Layers, lace. Hard knob one end, two sticks other end . . .

"A doll."

"Yup," he said. "Purtiest one I ever saw." He took it away from me. "Chip, hush now. Wait till the wind dies."

I waited in the whispering dark. The breeze was fitful, airless. It would drop to almost nothing, until all the other breathings and stirrings could be heard, and then giggle on up to be a breeze again. Suddenly, then, it was gone. From before us, in the pitch blackness, a yucca whispered.

"There she is," Grantham murmured. He stepped forword, and an unreasoning terror sent cold sweat oozing in my armpits. I stepped after him. He was leaning forward, apparently putting the doll into the lower swords of a young yucca.

Something touched my face and I bit my tongue. Then I realized that Grantham's heavy hand had tilted the plant toward us. Without conscious motivation I reached up swiftly and closed my hand on a flower. Without conscious reasoning I was very careful to twist it free without a sound or a detectible motion. I slipped it into my side pocket.

"'Bye, baby." He stood up and nudged me. "Let's go."

If anything, the way back was longer. I stumbled along behind him, wondering if he were sane enough to write that resignation coherently. When we reached the trail a loom of silver was staining the eastern sky.

"Easy going now," was all he said.

We trudged into the rising moon. I was deeply disturbed, but Grantham was calm and apparently deeply content.

The yuccas thinned, and we started up the valley's throat. Abruptly Grantham grunted and stopped.

"What is it?"

Silently he pointed. Fifty feet up the slope something wavered and flickered in the moonlight. "Bless her heart," he said. "Come on, Chip."

He struck off toward whatever it was, and I followed him, walking on the balls of my feet, my eyes too wide, so that they hurt.

When I caught up with him he stopped, turned to me, and drew his knife. "Symbiosis, Chip."

I don't think he could see my face, I wouldn't want to.

He dropped to one knee and I leaped backward, stood spraddled, gasping. I watched him digging carefully in the ground, while over and around him fluttered a silent cloud of small white moths. They were not yucca moths. I know they weren't because yucca moths never, never cluster near the ground. I mean, moths that cluster that way are not yucca moth, they aren't, they were not, they couldn't be.

Look it up if you don't believe it.

Grantham grunted, pulled, and up out of the ground came an object that looked like a large parsnip. "Ever see one of these in the flesh, Chip?"

Gingerly, I took it, squinted at it in the brightening moonlight. It was like a tuber, spineless, and with the upper end rounded and ribbed. I slipped my fingers along the grooves between the ribs and felt the small round protuberances.

"Lophophora," I said. My voice sounded odd to me. "I don't know which one."

"Doesn't matter." He trimmed off the grooved part and dropped it into his satchel. "Long as it's peyotl, who's quibbling?"

Back on the trail, I swallowed hard and asked, "That's symbiosis? You leave a doll on a yucca, and moths find peyotl for you?"

He laughed his big laugh. "You can't see farther than your nose," he said gaily and insultingly, "let alone as far as your front teeth."

"If you'll explain," I said stiffly, "I shall listen."

"The doll's a symbol," he said, suddenly deeply serious. "It represents something as vital as cellulose to a bacterium, or bacterial products to a termite. I didn't need to give the doll itself, except it was her birthday. Long as I bring what she needs—and I do."

"And it—she—I mean, you get peyotl out of it," I floundered. "That's no symbol. That's cash money."

"It is? What do I do with the money? Well, what?"

"Grubstake," I mumbled, frightened by his intensity.

"I sell it for just what I need, no more," he said. "And with it I stay out here and"—he chuckled—"study my references."

At the saloon Grantham wrote his resignation, and I was glad to see that it was written exactly as the old Grantham would have done it. I tucked it away safely. We dined heartily and slept in the same room back of the bar, and in the morning he helped me buy a horse. It was, therefore, not until I was out on the hot sand again that I had a chance to study my specimen.

I felt very good that morning. I was, of course, sorry for poor mad Grantham. On the other hand—what was the little moth that clustered over peyotl at night? Not the yucca moth, surely. Surely not.

I wondered what had happened to that strange, pathetic little girl. Wandered out in her blue polka-dot dress, to die among the yuccas, no doubt.

I studied the wilted flower as I rode. Poor Grantham! This was enough to tip any trained botanist over the edge—this freak, sport, mutant yucca. Who ever heard of a white yucca flower with a large blue patch on each petal?

The Waiting Thing Inside

THEODORE STURGEON and DON WARD

Delia Fox stood in the center of the saddle shed, her face pale, her thin lips sucked in and bitten on, invisible. The Circle F's steady rider, Vic Ryan, squatted on his tall heels with his back to the wall and laughed at her. "All right, all right—I'll raid, I'll gun out your nester." He laughed again. "But under orders." He aimed the stem of his pipe at her. "The boss's orders."

"You know he'll never!"

"If I raid, he will," said Ryan easily. "And he'll give me those orders right up to and includin' the minute I kick in that nester's shack door."

"You mean you want him to go with you?"

"That's about it."

"That's the same thing as saying you won't go."

Ryan shrugged and began to pack his pipe. "I reckon hell *could* freeze over."

She stamped to the door. "Catch a lot of folks with some heavy hauling to do, the day it does," she snapped, and went out.

Ryan took the pipe from his mouth and laughed again. He

was not a jovial man and his laughter was ugly; but it suited his mood.

Through the open door he could see across the yard—see Delia Fox, stiff-backed, furious, as she stamped into the house. She was thirty-eight years old, with a face five years older and a body twenty years younger, and time was when Vic Ryan used to look at that figure with something besides the familiarity of contempt. He peered back over the years at himself, and at her, and he wondered vaguely who those people were—the rawboned young cowboy who'd asked her to marry him, and the girl with ice in her eyes who had told him to own more than an old saddle and an iron skillet before he suggested such a thing to his betters. A long time ago . . . and never a word had he spoken to her since that wasn't strictly business. Yet he'd stayed, year in and year out, holding the Circle F together against all comers—against the weather, against lazy cowhands they had to put up with at the rates the Circle F paid, against drought, landslide, botflies, and even Delia's brother Roy.

At the thought of Roy he spat. Roy was younger than Delia, and that and his flabbiness were what had led Vic so far astray in the early days: Who could have guessed that it was Roy's ranch—lock, stock, and chopping block? It had been Delia who handled the money, made the decisions, hired and fired. "Better see to the south waterhole today, Vic," Delia would say, and Roy would chime in, "Yeah, Vic, go clean out the waterhole." Always her order, her brother's echo. So marry into it; you can't do nothing to the boss's relatives, but a no-good brother-in-law rates a boot in the tail right after the honeymoon. So Vic Ryan had tried it, and she had spat in his eye—Delia Fox, queen of the range, the bitch.

And a year afterward he'd fallen over Roy Fox on the town trail, belly-down and puking drunk, but bragging for all that. Vic had brought him home and slung him into bed, but not before Roy had dragged him into the parlor and showed him the will by which Roy Fox's father, the old fool, had made Roy sole heir to the Circle F.

Something had happened to Vic Ryan that night, something so deep that he couldn't name it if he wanted to. It had to do with a woman who'd refused him because he had so little, when all the time she had nothing; it had to do with a pig-eyed jelly-belly who'd order a better man to do jobs he wouldn't do himself, any time his sister wanted something done. Whatever it was, it made Vic Ryan stay, not planning—because the thing was planned; not building—because it was built . . . just waiting.

A long wait.

And a longer one yet, he chuckled, before she gets Roy Fox to ride out with me to raid that nester. The nester had squatted in the narrow eastern end of the valley. There was bottomland there, dark and fertile, and good water. Circle F stock had winter-grazed there for years, although legally it wasn't Circle F land. The nester, a heavy-set, towheaded stranger with a spavined wife and a rickety kid, hadn't sent any announcements around or even come calling; one fine day, there he was, with a dirty sod house and a plow and a team of oxen. Delia Fox wanted the nester out of "our" valley, boundary or no, and even if he was a full day's ride away. Vic Ryan wanted him out too, for somewhat less emotional reasons: he knew a successful squatter would bring another, and then fifty more, and goodbye free range. He took the trouble to ride into town and find out quietly if the nester had filed any sort of claim, and came back with the news that the nester had not—too busy, too lazy, or too ignorant; it didn't matter.

But Roy—Roy had shrugged when he heard about the nester, changed the subject when he heard about the claim (or lack of it), and when Delia started getting waspish about it, he started drinking. Vic Ryan understood. He knew it was only a matter of time before Delia would lay her ears back and *make* Roy do something about the nester, and the idea of facing up to a stranger was more than Roy could handle. One day he came into the bunkhouse, mottle-faced, red-eyed, and sat down on Vic's bunk. He started to call Vic a chummy "old boy" and Vic told him to get the hell off his clean blanket-roll and say what he had come to say. Roy said, "Sure, sure, boss," soothingly, and got up and stood weaving in the doorway, and suggested that Vic ride over to the east pass and see if some Circle F stock hadn't strayed up there, and on the way maybe warn off that nester, huh?

Vic told him to go do his own dirty work, whereupon Roy got up on his drunken dignity and said, "Damn it, Ryan, I can run things around here without you, you know."

Vic laughed in his face and told him yeah, but his sister couldn't.

But Roy had gone, all the same, and so had Vic Ryan. For at daybreak that next morning an infuriated Delia Fox had saddled up and galloped east, and a shaken and deflated Roy had crept into the bunkhouse to beg Vic Ryan to follow and stop her. For a long moment Vic stared at the quivering rancher and thought it over, and what tipped the scales he never knew, but he snatched up the fire-bucket, doused Roy Fox, and snarled at him to come on. They saddled up

and got their guns and rode, and it wasn't until afternoon
that they caught up with Delia. She had nothing to say to
them at all, but kept on riding east, and they followed.

When they crested the rise and saw, down by the cliffs,
the sod shack, Roy suddenly spurred up beside his sister
and said, "You really got nothing to say to that man, Dele.
We're off our land." He was chalky and shaking. Delia said
coldly, "You're the one to say it. If you can't find the words
in your head, get 'em out of this"—and she handed him a
bottle of whiskey from her saddlebag.

Vic Ryan, watching, felt all his scorn and disgust of Roy
Fox melt and slump into a puddle of pity: for the sight of
the bottle was a bigger thing to the man than any insult, and
Roy took it, drank a third of it without stopping, then looked
at his sister with his eyes streaming and told her she was a
peach.

They rode down the slope. What looked like a scarecrow
in the scratchy garden-patch froze and cowered and ran
bleating into the shack. That was the wife. What looked like
a small white ape scuttled in after her—that was the kid.
They rode on, passing the brush margins, and there were
the oxen, the plow, and the nester.

Roy took another drink. Vic Ryan got his carbine out of its
boot and laid it across his belt-buckle. He'd always liked a
carbine. Delia sucked in her lips.

The nester broke and ran, and Roy Fox laughed a rich,
deep man's laugh and spurred his horse. The nester turned
to look as he ran, his foot caught a clod, and over he went,
withers and rump. Roy let out a roar and a Rebel yell and
the nester scrambled to his hands and knees and leaped
downhill once, twice, three times like a huge hoptoad. Then

he was at the shack and inside, and the crazy split-rail and cowhide door banged shut.

The three Circle F riders cantered up and crowded the door. Roy's eyes were bright and his cheeks pink. "Outa your hole, gopher-boy!" he bellowed, and got maybe three syllables of the rich laugh out when the door swung again on its leather hinges and the nester stood there blinking at them. He was a big man, made even larger by the great mat of yellow hair and beard that surrounded his face, and by the tiny doorway that framed him. His thick left arm hung to the lintel above him, his right arm and shoulder were squeezed out of sight by the doorframe. Deep in Vic Ryan's mind was an indelible picture, and this man brought it blazing to him again: a bear he had once hamstrung with a bad shot, its useless hind legs crowded against a rock, its foreclaws flexing, its little eyes, dark but also incandescent, hurt and hating, reading Vic's face from side to side as it wagged its head; and it panted like this man—too fast, too hard, a harsh series of whispered moans.

"You got to get off this land, gopher-boy," Roy exulted, still full of downhill speed and whiskey.

Delia said, out of the side of her tight mouth, "Three weeks."

"Yeah, three weeks," Roy said.

"Or we'll be back," spat Delia.

"Yeah, back," said Roy, "with a keg of gunpowder and a—"

But just then the nester said hoarsely, "No!" and pulled out that right arm and hand; and in it was a single-barreled shotgun which, at that range, looked like a field-piece. "No," the man gasped, "you go." He moved the gun. "Go, you go." His own huge inhalation sucked his lips shut with an audible slap, and they could hear the rest of the breath hiss into his nostrils; he could say no more with words, but only with the mad hurt-animal eyes.

Roy Fox squeaked like a booted mouse and rocked back in the saddle, to wheel; but he jerked the lines so hard his horse squealed and reared high, staggering forward. The nester stood right under the flailing hoofs (and if he won't back up for that, thought Vic, he won't for anything on earth) until, for balance, the horse fell away sidewise, barely keeping its feet, and streaked away grunting and bleeding from the mouth, with Roy crouched low in the saddle and roweling away like a cyclist.

Delia's mount skittered and danced and then followed Roy's, less frantically. She cried, in the rusty, taut tones of a sparrowhawk, "Three weeks!" and let her horse gallop.

Vic Ryan cantered away from the shack slowly, half-turned in his saddle, his carbine ready, all his attention on the shack and none for his horse, which he knew would follow the others. He sat that way, cramped and concentrated for an uphill mile, and still the nester filled the doorway, the shotgun in his hands, and they filled the air with hate and fear, until the hill crest intervened and Roy could turn to find the others.

Roy was just throwing his empty bottle at a hornet's nest. He missed it. "I guess I told *him!*"

Delia didn't say anything. Vic blew, short and sharp, from his nostrils, so hard he hurt his ears, but he didn't say anything either.

They rode three miles and camped, and in the morning dark, Vic rose and left them. He got back two hours before they did, kicked the hell out of Kewkie, one of the worthless drifting cowhands they had to hire, and got some sleep in the bunkhouse . . .

And now the three weeks were gone, and three days more, and Delia was trying to get him to go raid the nester and gun him out. She loco? he thought wonderingly. Seen her hot after things before—might's well try to turn a stampede with a willow switch; but nothing like this nester business, the way she's got her ears laid back. Vic shook his head slowly, rose and stretched, and went to bed.

It was the darkest predawn when he jolted up to a roaring and chattering. He sat up grunting, peering at the color of the night through the open door, sorting out the time of day from the noises he heard, then sleepily pulling the noises apart. It was Roy Fox, charging around the bunkhouse in the dark and calling him. He heard the flat of a hand strike flesh, and Roy's roar, "There you are, Ryan! Come up out of there," and the whimper, "It's me, Kewkie, Mr. Fox."

"I'm over here," growled Vic, and his nose confirmed what his ears had told him: Roy Fox was crazy drunk.

"Well, come on," Roy yelled. "We got a chore to do." He started one of his Rebel yells but got to coughing.

"Come on where?"

Roy Fox aimed himself at Vic's voice. "You told Dele you'd take my orders, right from here to that gopher hole?"

"The nester. My God, Roy—"

"Put up or shut up. You got my orders, you'll have 'em all the way. Come on now, jump, damn you! I'm go' git me a yella pelt and nail it up in the honeywell an' use it to—"

"Your sister ready to ride?"

"What you think I am? This here's a *man's* chore. She can stay here and keep house."

"Well, hell just froze over," muttered Vic. He pulled on

his Levi's and hung on the holster. He saw it all—his flat refusal to do this job unless Roy bossed it, Delia's determination to find some way, somehow, to make it happen. Enough of her rasping nag, enough firewater, enough—well, that would be enough. He sighed and got his hat. "Come on then."

They saddled up and rode.

Within the first hour Vic Ryan was so heartily sick of the whole project, and everything and everyone connected with it, that it took an effort of will not to cut away and head straight over the mountains to the south, leaving the valley forever. He had help, however, in keeping the course with Roy. It was that thing within him, waiting all these years, waiting for a certain something from Roy, a certain something from Delia. It had divined that he need not wait much longer.

It had better not be much longer.

Roy's voice went on and on in the dimming dark, exultant, laced with that rich, deep laughter, avid, eager. ". . . woman's fine in a kitchen and not too bad with her nose in a ledgerbook, but the fightin' and the ridin's not for them. You been the places I been, Vic ol' hick"—this brought on a paroxysm of alcoholic appreciation from its author, but nothing from the audience—"you learn about ladies. They have feelin's. Sensibilities. Now that nester froggin' an' hoppin' down the hill, they can see a thing like that and only laugh." He laughed. "But the job we're gonna do, a little hollerin' when we stick 'em, a little red ink splashed around—you know—we wouldn't want the ladies in on that. For men's work—*men*," he boomed. He got the cork out of a bottle with his teeth. "The ladies, bless 'em!" He gurgled and went *ahh* shrilly; the sound recalled to Ryan the hoarse panting of the nester (or was it the hamstrung bear?). In revulsion he learned, on the instant, a trick of voluntary deafness, so that the universe contracted to the trail jerkily unrolling under the horses' hoofs, sealed seethings from that impatient thing inside of him, and Roy Fox's voice became just a drone conveying nothing.

When next he tuned in the voice, the melody had changed. "You'd never know it to look at me," Roy was saying sorrowfully, "but I'm a man of culture, having received, back East, an enviable education, among people among whom, my sickly-hickly friend, you'd be lost among . . ."

"Give me a drink, Roy," said Vic, and took the proffered bottle and hurled it against a rock. "By gosh, it slipped right out of my hand," he said.

Roy Fox looked deeply injured. "I shall not chastise you for that, Ryan. I shall simply withhold my gentlemanly instincts and refrain from sharing the next bottle with any such piebald pismire as you." He broke out another bottle, drank, and dramatically corked it. Ryan disconnected him again, and lapsed into the jogging miasma he had just invented.

The growling of his stomach at length became noisy enough, and a midmorning sun high enough, to call him back to an earth on which he had saddled up without breakfast. He pulled up and dismounted.

"Whassamatta?" Roy wanted to know.

"Eat something," said Vic shortly.

"I give the orders around here," said Roy Fox in an ugly voice.

"Order us to pull up and spread some chuck then," said Ryan wearily.

"Very well," said Roy with a grand wave of the hand.

"You will halt here an' prepare shushtenance." He fell off his horse.

Ryan let him lie there and got a fire going. He broke out some Arbuckle coffee, put it in a can, filled it from the nearby brook, and set it on a flat stone in the fire to boil. He tore up some sourdough bread and put some bacon in the skillet. Then he stepped over Fox's prone figure and went through the man's saddlebags. He found one bottle, two-thirds gone. He put it back. He saw to his disgust that the man's rifle boot was empty; on a hunch he felt down inside it and found a pint flask of whiskey. He hurled it away into the woods. Then he bent over Roy Fox and pulled him to a sitting position.

"Come on, Roy. Soup's on." Fox merely mumbled incoherently and hung his head; when Ryan released him he sagged like a half-bag of oats. Ryan cursed and went back to the fire and ate.

For two endless hours Roy lay like that, defying shouts, slaps and the smell of the powerful coffee. At last Ryan squatted on his heels and did nothing but wait. When Fox stirred at last, Ryan arose, grunting from pins-and-needles in his legs, and got the can of coffee. He handed it over without a word, and Roy Fox bent his head over the fumes. Without drinking any, he set the can down delicately and said in an apologetic tone, "Li'l eye-opener, y'know?" and pulled himself up beside his horse. He found the remaining third of a bottle, drank it thirstily, and said in a strong clear voice, "Now for some of that coffee—go just right." He sank to his knees, sipped twice, then gulped down the coffee. He was quite still for a time, then threw up his head, belched loudly, started at the sound, and looked all around him. "Where am I?"

Ryan told him. Told him why, too.

Roy Fox just shook his head, wondering, disbelieving, denying—Ryan could not know. Ryan swung up on his horse. "Well, let's get it over with."

Roy Fox hesitated, then slowly followed suit.

They rode in silence for another hour, and then Fox began fumbling in his clothes, his saddlebags, even the rifle boot. Once was not enough; he searched again and again. At last he spurred up beside Ryan. "Got any whiskey, Vic?"

"No."

Roy fell back again. For another hour, silence. Once Ryan thought he heard weeping, but he could not bring himself to turn. Then, "Vic!"

Ryan moved over to the side of the trail to allow Fox to ride up, but he did not. "Vic?" he called again.

Ryan cursed, wheeled, and cantered back. "Now what the hell?"

Fox wet his lips. "What we want with that nester? What's he done to us?"

"What's botherin' you, Roy?"

"Valley's too small, him and us? Outside our land, takes a whole day to ride between . . ."

His voice expressing a patience he did not feel, Vic Ryan said softly, "What's the matter, Roy? What do you want to do?"

"Well, I don't know what the hell we're doing out here."

"Afraid Gopher-boy'll take your ear off with his shotgun?"

"That ain't it!" snapped Roy.

"You're like a steam train, Roy—you can carry just so much to stoke yourself with and when that's gone you quit."

"What are you talking about?"

"Guts. Whiskey."

"Now look, damn it, I give the orders and you don't ask why. Didn't you come out on my orders—didn't I tell you you'd have my orders all the way?"

"That was the arrangement." The waiting thing inside him fairly hummed with tension.

"Well," said Roy Fox smugly, "you'll ride back to the Circle F, starting now, with me, and that's an order." He turned his horse and started along the backtrail.

"Yes, sir, boss," said Vic Ryan, and drew his carbine, and shot Roy Fox through the head. Fox stiffened, made an ineffectual gesture with both hands, and fell forward. His horse started slightly and then began to jog toward the Circle F. Ryan spurred his mount and he began to gallop, also toward the Circle F. "Yes, sir." Ryan said again. He drew alongside the other horse and caught the jouncing body just as it was about to slide off. "Whoa," he crooned, and both horses stopped.

Ryan dropped off, still supporting the corpse, and it was only then that the rage overcame him—a flood, a flame of it. Or perhaps it had been there all along, and only now emerged where he could see it.

Finally it washed by, leaving the husk of that waiting thing inside him, and some dull lumpy leavings at the bottom of it. It was this he had waited for, all these years, and what all the years of waiting had been for. All that was left was this nameless lump of leftovers. He'd scour that out too —he knew he would; he knew it couldn't be cleaned out here, but he *knew* he'd do it.

Time enough—time enough for all that. He was used to waiting for the time to come. He turned the body belly-down across the saddle and snugged it with a lariat, shoulders to ankles, under the cinch. Finished, he stopped to

watch a mosquito treading the dead man's neckerchief
with its delicate feet as it slowly made its way to the strip of
flesh that showed between silk and denim; then he swung
up into the saddle.

He was asleep when he reached the Circle F. It was after
sundown, raining a little, and he awoke slumped in the saddle, with the dark bulks of house, bunkhouse, saddle shed,
and barn about him in the yard. He climbed down stiffly and
for a moment leaned his head against the arch of the horse's
neck. His eyes closed and he very nearly slept again; he had
never in his life been this tired. He straightened his back and
struck himself roughly on the cheekbones with the palms of
his cold wet fists, and turned to on the wet knots of the lariat.
He pulled the body by its shoulders and it slid off into the
mud while he respectfully held the head high enough so it
wouldn't go down too. It was a respect indicating only how
completely through he was with Roy Fox; he had nothing
left for him—no vengeance, not even disgust. He dragged
the body into the saddle shed and turned it over on its back
in the dark there. He went out and shut the door and returned to the horses. He turned them into the corral and
threw the saddles into the bunkhouse. He didn't know what
he was doing, but he didn't have to. He hadn't been able to
see in the saddle shed either, and he hadn't needed to.

Someone came in. A lantern. "Vic?"

"Yuh."

She said, "Where's Roy?"

"Saddle shed."

The lantern went away. He turned to where he had
thrown the saddles on the floor and kicked them with his
boot toe. The lantern came back. "What are you going to
do?"

"Sleep."

He stumbled away, but her hand held him. She said, "Don't stay out here, Vic." She led him to the woodshed, which adjoined the pantry connecting with the kitchen, and then across a floor and around a corner and through a door. The bed there was softer than a bed ought to be, but he was conscious hardly long enough to be aware of that . . .

Being dead turned the saddle shed into pale blue paint and a crazy-quilt, chintz, rag rugs, and a spool rocker . . . how was old Ryan making out in the house?

Then a slight sound from the doorway chased the dream, and he wasn't Roy Fox lying lifeless in the saddle shed but Vic Ryan lying here looking at—he clutched the quilt to his bare chest and gasped like a schoolgirl.

"It's all right," said Delia, coming in.

He had never seen her this way. Her hair, no longer skull-tight and bunned, was parted in the middle, and two braids framed her face. She wore a close-fitting robe with a huge skirt right down to the floor, and it was the palest pink at the top and gradually got to be scarlet at the bottom. She had lip-rouge on, too, but that wasn't clamped tight and sucked in any more. She walked over to the bed and sank down on the floor until their heads were at a level and all he could see of her garment was the pale pink part. He cast a nervous glance over her head at the door.

"It's all right," she said again. "There's nobody around but us."

"What about Kewkie?"

"I sent him to town to tell the sheriff about Roy."

He tried to swallow but there wasn't anything to swallow. His mouth was dry as an alkali flat in a droughty August. "Tell him *what* about Roy?"

"How he got killed."

Vic Ryan didn't say anything.

"Got killed fighting with the nester," she amended.

His mouth opened and breath rushed in, but nothing could come out because of the cool hand she laid on it. "It makes everything come out right," she said. He wished she would talk without fixing her eyes so hard on him; he felt like a skunk pitchforked to a henhouse wall. She got larger, or moved closer, he couldn't tell which. "Vic . . ." she said.

He wanted something of this woman, and he couldn't name the thing he wanted. He knew, though, what he didn't want. "Where's my clothes?"

"Vic," she whispered.

"Where's my clothes?" She was still for so long that he turned to look at her. "Well?"

"I'll get them," she said in a low voice. She rose and turned with one motion so that she did not face him again. He lay looking out the window, eastward down the valley, and the only thought he could capture was something that couldn't matter now: Roy had been the only one at Circle F who didn't care if the nester came or went.

He heard the soft *plath* of cloth on wood, but did not turn his head until he heard the door close. Then he rose and for the first time in years dressed from neck to toenails in clean, ironed, mended garments. He found his boots by the bed—not the ones he had worn last night, but dry ones from the bunkhouse, all scraped and oiled.

He stepped out into the kitchen. Hot coffee steamed in a china mug beside a platter of eggs and bacon, a bowl of butter with the paddle-marks still on it, and bread that had to be oven-new, for he could smell it. "Dig in," she said.

He wondered why she had to speak before he could notice that she had changed while he was dressing; she now wore a simple, starched house dress with bright little strawberries and green leaves printed over it. He had seen her in it before, but never with her hair this way and her mouth all different. He sat down before the food, and saliva squirted so heartily he felt pain under his tongue.

"You sure fix everything the way it should be."

She shot him a quick look. "Everything?"

He ate, thinking hard about eating; but pretty soon he'd eaten it all, so he had to say, "Roy's dead. Ain't things a little cheery around here?"

"Yes!" she said fiercely.

"All right," he said. He watched her picking up dishes, the way she moved. "You thought right away it was the nester done it?"

"Anybody would think so—why not? Didn't he threaten us all with a gun? I was there. I remember. You were there. Besides, he's just a squatter and Roy had the right to drive him out."

"I tell my story, you tell yours, and everything's all straightened out."

"Yes," she said. Suddenly she smiled at him. He didn't like it. She asked, "Thought about what you'll do then?"

He hadn't but he did now, and there was no hesitation. "I'm going to get just as far away from here as I can get."

She came quietly and sat down opposite him at the table. "You wouldn't do that." She was gazing at him the way she had in the bedroom; he could feel it like heat on his lowered eyelids.

He muttered, "I couldn't stay here without . . . with just the two of us. People would . . . it wouldn't be right."

"It could be right, if—"

Slowly he raised his eyes. Hers were fixed on her hands, which turned and churned and pressed each other, trembling. Abruptly he laughed. "I still don't have but a saddle and a skillet!"

She colored. "Oh . . . you remember everything, don't you?" Suddenly she took his hand. It burned him. She said, "Can't you see it's all different now? I have all this—everything. And besides, you never could understand: it wasn't me who turned you down, it was Roy. Roy wouldn't chance a better man as a relative. If I'd married you, he'd have thrown us both out, or burned down the place if we wouldn't go. That was the one thing he prided himself on all these years—keeping you on, keeping us apart."

"I still don't have nothing."

"You do! You do! Or you would . . . I have the Circle F, but you have me!" she cried.

And now, only now, he knew what else it was that had been waiting—waiting all these years deep inside him—part and parcel of the thing he had relieved on the trail yesterday. "Ask me right out."

"Wh-what?"

"Ask me," he said. Something began to pulse, to kick. "Ask me what you want."

"I don't—"

"I'm going to roll my blanket," he said. "I'll leave as soon as—"

"Marry me," she whispered, and lowered her face to her arm.

He laughed. "I can't hear you."

"Marry me."

"Beg me."

"Why you—you . . ."

She stood up and looked down at his laughing face. "I do, Victor—I beg you marry me."

And that was the other thing, and that was all. His secret place closed down on itself with its secrets gone, and he could feel it healing; and he yelled, "*NO, by God!*"

When he looked at her face he was frightened. He sidled up off the bench, his eyes on her like those of a hypnotized bird, and backed off a safe two paces. For moments they hung like that, and then there was the thump and rumble of horses, and they turned to stare out at the yard. The sheriff, three deputies, the coroner, Kewkie. They dismounted, and went where Kewkie pointed—the saddle shed.

Delia's voice, when she spoke, had the frightening overtones of that hawk's shriek Vic had heard the day they warned the nester. She said, "Better have your story straight when they come in. It's got to be the same now as at the trial."

"I'm not worried."

"You should be," she said. "When we cornered the nester he ran for his gun. What he brought out must have been the only gun he had—a shotgun. Roy wasn't killed by a shotgun."

"All this time you—"

"I could testify the nester had a carbine," she said coolly. "And if you did too it would be the word of both of us against the nester. I'd be glad to testify that way, Vic, if you wanted me to."

"Well, I want you to."

"Matter of fact, there's a way to keep me from testifying against you—ever."

Steps on the porch, knuckles on the door. "Yes," he said

blackly. "I know three ways." He turned his back on her and opened the door.

"Howdy, Vic. Miss Fox."

"Howdy, Sheriff. You been in the saddle shed?"

"A second," said the sheriff. He was a gray little man with what looked like brand-new eyes. "Doctor's in there now. I saw all I needed. Sorry, Miss Fox."

Delia clasped her hands together, watching Vic Ryan. "Did you get the nester?" she asked the sheriff.

"He's safe and snug in the jailhouse," said the sheriff.

Vic's eyes met Delia's. With sudden, profound composure she inquired, "Well, what can we do for you now, Sheriff?"

"Just tell me what you know," said the sheriff. "Miss Fox? Vic?"

"I'll give you mine first," said Vic Ryan tautly. To Delia, he said, "Marrying you is the first way. This here's the second."

"What?" asked the sheriff.

"Nothing. Something we were talking about when you came in. Sheriff, I killed Roy Fox—shot him going away, on the trail. That nester, he didn't have but a shotgun."

Delia Fox screamed.

The sheriff blinked. "Well, that's enough to start out with. I'll have to have your gun, Vic."

"The carbine? It's in the bunkhouse. Or were you talking about this one?" and he unholstered his Colt and held it so it pointed exactly on the bowknot on the cotton belt of Delia Fox's starched house dress. "This here's the third way," he said softly.

Nobody breathed for a time. Then the sheriff said, "You better stop playing around now, Vic."

"Sure," said Vic, and handed him the gun. "I wouldn't shoot you, Delia. You're dead already. I hope you live to be a hundred and twelve and spend it countin' your money."

Delia Fox cast her eyes in one wide arc, taking in the shabby Circle F, its people, all its shabby years. She gasped, "But the nester—"

"Oh, that nester, sure," said the sheriff grimly. "You know, folks, I'd give a good deal to hear the story you were about to tell just now . . . guess I never will, and it don't really matter any more. The nester—I got him in jail all right. Had him there three days, going on four, tucked in safe and snug with his wife and kid. That's where he wanted to be, so we let him. You folks scared the chips out that pore farmer; he wouldn't've stayed on his little spread past your deadline to save his everlastin'."

Delia covered her face.

Vic Ryan said, "Roy would've been real proud."

The sheriff said, "So you see how perplexin' it was to be keepin' a man in the jailhouse for his own protection, and then have someone ride in with the rumor he'd killed Roy Fox fifty miles away."

Delia whispered, "Vic, please—"

"Come on," said Vic Ryan to the sheriff. "Whatever she's got to say, I'd still rather hang." Inside, he felt good, the way a man must if he has everything, has done everything, he ever really wanted.

The Man Who Figured Everything

THEODORE STURGEON and DON WARD

This is about Jim Conlin the Badlands Bookkeeper. He was, according to the journals of the time, a terror, a menace, and a scourge. He was, in the flesh, a mild man, young and balding early, with diffident horizontal lines across his brow.

He hid in the hills with his half-dozen riders, all but one of whom outweighed him, but then that one was only a three-quarter breed Nez Percé, and hardly counted. These men, each to his taste, fought and gambled, drank and wenched, always providing they had Jim Conlin's advance permission and pursued the hobby somewhere away from Jim Conlin's hideout. A long way away. There was a town, Dead Mole Spring, eight miles away as the crow flies, where nobody had ever seen Conlin or any of his crew—a good example of the way the Bookkeeper of the Badlands arranged things.

Jim Conlin figured. He figured everything, the Bookkeeper did. He never moved until he was ready, and when he was ready, it was altogether. In some sleepy mountain town, just when the marshal was out and the sheriff drunk, and the bank heavy with cowpokes' pay and prospectors' dust, Jim Conlin's men would whirl up out of the ground like dust devils and be gone like smoke, the gold with them.

The only similarity between one job and another was that element of perfect planning, perfect timing—the only clue, most of the time, as to who the robbers were. Unless, of course, Conlin wanted it otherwise, like the time he took the Rocky Summit Bank three times in one week, just because everybody was so positive he wouldn't be back.

He would have been caught for sure the time rumors got around that he was going to rob the express between Elwood and Casson's Quarry; the train was loaded with law and the tracks lined on both sides with one of the biggest posses the West had ever seen, which was fine with Conlin, who was busy at the time robbing another train on another railroad.

He would certainly be remembered in large type, like Butch Cassidy and the James boys, if it were not for his concentration on fine detail—this got him only into fine print. As a man, he was colorless to the point of invisibility; as a desperado he was too methodical to be remembered. Probably the largest two reasons his reputation has faded with the newspapers of his day were these: he never killed a lawman, and he was never caught.

There came one night to Jim Conlin's hideout, Arch Scott, invited and escorted. Scott had something of a reputation locally: cautious, sober, with special skills in safes and lockboxes. He could use a gun, and didn't, which was a high recommendation to the Bookkeeper; and Scott's ability to do nine consecutive jobs with the methods of nine different people clinched it.

Although the Bookkeeper occasionally took on a brace or

two of drifters for special jobs, letting them go afterwards, he liked to keep a half-dozen regulars with him; and there was a vacancy just now, one Farley Moore having succumbed to romance. (That was Conlin's name for it; actually it was tetanus, contracted after a Rocky Summit housewife, mistaken for a doxie by Moore, removed his ear with an iron skillet.)

So Conlin gave Arch Scott his guided tour and his most careful examination, introducing him around, watching him, making his estimate. He liked Scott—liked him, that is, the way a man likes a well-made saddle or a clean rifle. The Bookkeeper had human feelings, but he had a place for them, and he kept them all there. Which introduces Loretta Harper.

She was the only woman permitted at the hideout, except for a few squaws who washed clothes and swept out. Conlin had found her working in a place she was glad to get out of—especially with a man who knew enough about her to ask no questions and saw to it that she got more of the things she liked than she could hope for working in town. He had something for all her hungers but one, and that one was beyond his comprehension. It was beyond hers, too, until Arch Scott came.

"This here's Loretta," Conlin said when he brought Scott in, and Scott saw a carving come to life, silk and ivory and ice, as out of place here as a leaf from *Godey's Lady's Book* tacked to a haybarn; and Loretta saw a neat man with heavy shoulders and good teeth and eyes you couldn't keep secrets from.

And that should have been that. It would have been, as far as Arch was concerned. He was there on business, and business came first. And Loretta felt nothing, just then; Jim

Conlin's men came and went and his steady crew was always there. This was another one, only another one. As Conlin and Scott left she turned back to her mirror, and if anyone had asked her, she probably wouldn't have remembered the new man's name.

Conlin and Arch Scott went down the mountain for fifty yards or so to the cabin and went in. "Henry Little Hawk," said Conlin, nodding at the slight figure squatting by the door.

"Howdy," said Scott. "I'm—"

"Yuh," grunted the little man. He looked like an animated piece of mahogany, and seemed to be composed mainly of eyebrows, nose, and sharp shinbones.

Conlin chuckled. "He knows who you are. He's the one found you for me. Or anyway, he's the one who found out it was really you who did the jobs you say you done. He sees everything and everybody, Henry does, and nobody sees him." He went to the back wall of the cabin and put his boot on it. It swung aside. "Havin' Henry around's like having your eyes out on stalks forty mile long," he said, motioning Scott through the opening, then closing it. "Only a misfit Nez Percé breed, but God what a memory! Look at a town he never saw before, ride all night, draw you a map so fine you could go there and jump over a yaller dog blindfold."

They were standing at one end of a section mine tunnel, with the wooden cabin wall behind them and a rockfall at the other end. The long room was fitted out like a bunkhouse, but with a fire in the center, its smoke curling upward to be lost in a fissure overhead. All evidence of the old mine workings had been carefully removed from the outside and the weather-beaten cabin, scarcely large enough for two men, substituted. Any posseman willing to believe the evidence of his own eyes would call you a liar if you told him you had seen a bunch the size of Conlin's disappear into this hillside. Not that a posse had ever been within miles of this place, of course.

"Can sleep eleven here in a pinch," Conlin said. "Ain't but four now—Henry, he don't bunk here. Suit you?"

Scott swept the place with a glance. "Fine, Conlin. I slept in worse and paid money for it. Where's the—"

He was interrupted by a blast of language, English and Spanish, profane and obscene, packed tight as grapeshot and twice as loud. A tall man, hidden until now by the end bunks, sprang to his feet, snatching a coiled bullwhip from a peg on the rock wall. He was a blaze of color and fancywork, Mexican weaving and tooled leather. On his shoulder blades, held by an elaborately braided thong, perched a hand-blocked silken felt worth six months' of a cowpoke's pay.

He shook out the whip and brought it whistling back, and in that split second Conlin was behind him, grasping the lash. The whip flicked out of the man's hand and Scott, still standing by the wooden wall, had to step aside to avoid the loaded handle.

"Now, Al, you know better'n that," said Conlin quietly. He drew up beside the bunks and looked down. A blanket was spread on the floor, and on it was gold money and a deck of cards. A second giant knelt by the blanket, scowling. His eyes were red, very small, very wide apart, and at the moment full of kill. Conlin's appearance had arrested him halfway to his feet with a nickel-plated .45 halfway out. He came to his feet now, but slowly, and when he stopped moving, his gun was holstered and his hand clear of it.

The man with the fancy hat, Al, began to splutter at Conlin, something about wart-hogs, something about an inside straight, something in Spanish. Conlin shook his head gently, stooped, and picked up most of the cards. Deftly he stacked them, cut them, and tore the pack in two, letting the pieces flutter to the ground.

The two big men watched the pieces fall. The red-eyed man bit his lower lip silently with square yellow teeth. The other one ran out of splutter and simply stood there, breathing hard. If Arch Scott expected anything else to happen, he was disappointed. Conlin motioned to him and said, "Scott, this here's Big Ike Friend." The red-eyed man glowered at the stranger. "And Al Coe."

"Arch Scott. Howdy."

"Howdy," Coe grunted. He walked past the others and went for his whip. He came back, coiling it as he walked, not looking at anybody, and hung it on the peg. "Seen you before, Scott," he said with his back turned.

"Don't think so."

"Ever down Taos way, or 'Dobe?"

"I come from the Dakotas," said Arch Scott quickly, "where folks don't ask questions."

Big Ike Friend produced a harsh brief snicker from the depths of his flat nose.

"Tell you something," said Conlin in a voice so mild in the sudden tension that Scott nearly jumped with shock. "We don't fight among ourselves here. Anybody wants to rassle, go pick on a stranger some place else. You ain't learned that, Scott, and you and Big Ike forgot it, I guess, Al. We don't gamble here, we don't drink—not enough to get drunk on anyways—and there ain't no women allowed. I got nothing against them three things, but they're the three best reasons for fightin', and that kind of fightin' is one thing

I ain't got time to keep books on. Scott, you need anything, you ask Big Ike or Al Coe here. I'm going back to the house.

And he did, without so much as a good night, leaving all the makings of a three-sided donnybrook. But then Arch Scott laughed—not at the two big men, but in an indefinable way with them, so that he was no longer a stranger, but part of a crew which had just seen a hundred and forty pounds of mild logic putting out a fire. Big Ike laughed too; Al Coe did not, but he relaxed visibly.

"Where do I bunk?" Scott asked.

Big Ike pointed out the empties. Scott selected one and sat down on it, looking quizzically at the others. "How does he do it?"

"By bein' right," said Al Coe reluctantly.

"Lots of hombres go around being right, nobody listens," said Big Ike.

"Those are the guys that don't pay off," said Coe. "Bein' right is nothin' by itself."

And there it was, in as neat a nutshell as anyone could pack it. There's no point in disagreeing with a man who's always right, who also put money in your sock.

Arch Scott fell asleep that night knowing he wouldn't be bothered.

The horses were corraled in a narrow dry gulch a quarter of a mile away, visible from two places—inside, and straight up. Like the rest of the spread, it was only another scar on the hillside.

Conlin went down there in the morning with Loretta, to cut out a gentle horse for her. It was early, but Arch Scott was already up and about, standing just inside the narrow throat of the gulch, his hands in the back pockets of his Levi's and his hat on the back of his head. "Morning."

Conlin nodded to him. Loretta didn't say anything. Scott glanced at her, then took his hands out of his pockets and removed his hat. His tardiness was understandable. When Loretta rode, the carven goddess was folded up and put away. She wore Levi's and a shirt and a soft leather vest, and her bright hair was hidden under a wide-brimmed man's hat; and from twenty paces she looked like a country boy out to bark squirrels, which was the idea.

She stood by the rails near Scott and waited while Conlin went in with a bridle over his shoulder and a rope on one arm. Scott glanced at her once, but she seemed to be watching Conlin, so he said nothing. He watched Conlin too, and he liked what he saw.

The Bookkeeper did what he had to do without waste motion, and better than anyone he might have ordered to do it for him. He took a roan gelding on the first cast, reeled him in, and had the rope off and the bridle on in what looked like one movement. He led the animal to a shed by the rocky wall of the cut and went in for a saddle.

"Scott."

Arch looked at the woman. She had not moved, and was certainly not looking his way. Her voice had been just loud enough to reach him. He sensed that this was no casual approach to a casual conversation, so he took her cue and stayed where he was. "Ma'am?"

"Waterhole called Green Spring," she said, hardly moving her lips. In spite of its softness she had a surprisingly full voice. "Find it. Be there at two o'clock." Before he could answer or acknowledge, she had slipped through the rails and was walking toward Conlin.

He watched her mount and wheel the horse. He gathered his wits and dropped the bars for her as she rode out. She passed as if he did not exist. Scott replaced the bars without looking after her.

"We're going out on a little job today," Conlin told him when he came up.

"We are?"

"We are—Henry and me and Al and Big Ike. Moko and Gus, that's the two you ain't met yet, they're waiting for us."

"I do something wrong?"

Conlin seemed to think the question quite natural. "Hardly had a chance yet, have you?"

"What do you want me to do while you're out?"

Conlin swept out his arm in a wide circular motion. "Smell out this spread. I want you to memorize every rock and bush and cut and hogback within ten miles of here. They say a couple big glaciers carved up this country, Scott—I wouldn't know about that myself; but whoever done it was working for us. You'll see. You'll find out that this country can lose a Injun tracker with a pack o' hounds, if you know where to go. Nobody ever trailed us in here, and nobody's about to, because every man of us comes and goes a different way and knows a hundred more. You got to get to know this country like the inside of your front teeth."

"All right," Scott said.

Conlin laughed at his expression. "Don't get yourself so damn' disappointed, Scott. You're about to make the easiest money you'll ever make with us. You get a half share of everything we make, just for stayin' here. The other boys get one share each. I get two and a half. Your pay is free and clear. I got all the expenses. Understand?"

"Sounds fine to me."

"Long as you understand, there ain't nothin' to argue about, with me or anybody. You want to know anything, don't wonder and don't start rumors. Ask."

"All right," said Scott. He wet his lips. "Where you going today?"

Conlin laughed again. "He wants to know where we're goin', Henry."

From midair, apparently, came an amused grunt. Scott whirled and looked right, looked left, then looked up. Henry Little Hawk squatted on a rock ledge ten feet off the ground, toasting his sharp nose and his sharper shinbones in the morning sun. "God!" said Scott. "I never saw him up there."

"I told you before. Henry goes everywhere, nobody ever sees him."

Scott looked again at the little breed, who was slowly coming to life, crabbing sidewise down the bluff. Had he heard Loretta speak to him? And if so—what? Was this her hard luck, or Scott's, or Conlin's? Or maybe it didn't matter. Henry Little Hawk wouldn't be around at two this afternoon anyway.

Scott wrenched his mind away from these thoughts and said, "So where you say you're going?"

Again that amused syllable from Henry Little Hawk. Conlin said, "Tell you what, you ask Big Ike." He turned away and went back to the saddle shed. Scott watched him rope another horse and then went slowly back to the hidden bunkhouse. Al Coe was sitting at a deal table with the guts of one of his pearl-handled .45s spread out on a clean white cloth. For all his fancy-work, this man knew his weapons and treated them right. "Big Ike around?"

"Down to the corral," said Coe.

"I was just there."

Coe shrugged.

"Going to use those today," said Scott about the guns. It was the kind of statement that is a question.

Coe shrugged again and went on working.

Scott said suddenly, "Do I bother you?"

Coe seemed not to hear at all; and then Scott noticed his hands had stopped moving. He sat like that for a long moment, then slowly turned a pair of frozen eyes to take in the newcomer, from his hat to his hands, his holster, the plain strong boot on a bench, the knee on which Scott's crossed forearms rested. In a long, easy half whisper Al Coe said "No-o-o . . ." Scott might have said it the same way if someone had asked him if he was afraid of mice.

Scott smiled and said, "Too bad." He straightened up and went out, not hurrying. He knew that something had started that would have to be finished, and he regretted it; there were plenty of other things to worry him. Being liked or disliked by a jaybird like Al Coe didn't matter; just why, though, might matter very much. One possible reason might matter so much that Arch Scott would wind up dead.

Outside he watched a squaw, a misplaced Pueblo, laboring up the hill toward him from the ramshackle cookhouse, carrying two buckets of what had to be hot breakfast. From the direction of the corral he saw Big Ike swinging along the hillside. Scott let the squaw go on inside and stood where he was, though his stomach wanted to follow her; he was hungry and those buckets smelled good. "Mornin'," he said to the big man when he came up.

Big Ike nodded. Scott said, "Was down to the corral a while back, talked to Conlin."

"Talked to Conlin, did you?"

"Said you were ridin' out today."

"Said that, did he?"

"Asked him where to, he said you'd tell me."

"No, he didn't," said Big Ike. He would have gone on inside, but Scott caught his elbow. Big Ike stopped, freed his arm, and slowly wiped it with his other hand, as if Scott had left mud on it.

Scott said, "You don't want to tell me, Ike, say so."

Big Ike looked surprised. "Hell," he said placatingly, "don't go jumping salty. I wasn't there, but I bet a empty ca'tridge to a dollar that Conlin didn't say no such a thing." As Scott's eyes narrowed he delivered up a surprising, jovial grin and held up both his hands. "Tell you why. Ain't none of us knows where we're goin' till we git there. Conlin he always works like that."

"So why the hell didn't he say so?"

"You know as much about that as I do. He had a reason —he figures everything. Maybe he just wanted you to remember this special."

"The son!" said Scott, rueful and admiring.

"Yeah, he got his ways o' doin' things," chuckled Big Ike. "Now, what was it he reely said?"

"You're right," said Scott. "All he said was, if I want to know where you're ridin' today, ask Big Ike. He didn't say you'd tell me."

"He didn't even say I knew. Come on in and eat. You get a little tetchy when you're hungry, I can see that."

They went in to the buckwheat cakes and muscular black coffee the squaw had laid out. Al Coe had nothing to say to him.

Everybody but Arch Scott rode out at about nine o'clock.

They rode east, but in these hills that could mean anything. Scott wished he knew where they were going.

At noon he was picking his way up a creek, crossing and recrossing and letting one of Conlin's surefooted mountain ponies find the route. The Green Spring, he had been told, was the source of this particular stream. He had been told this by the Pueblo, who answered his question in Spanish. He had pretended not to understand her; he didn't want anyone to add his knowledge of Spanish to Al Coe's guess— if it was a guess—about Taos. So she had answered in English and he was now on his way. To what he didn't know, but he had shaved first.

He had to leave the creek at an alder thicket and cut out to open ground. He was well up into the hills now, and could see the rolling country for miles. Ahead of him, a steep slope was capped by a rocky cliff, mostly sheer, in some places overhanging. "That spring better be under the cliff," he muttered. "Sure won't get over it without wings."

He moved back to the stream when he could, and found it boiling along, large as ever. Well, maybe it ran along the base of the cliff . . .

But it didn't. He swore helplessly when he saw how it gushed right out of the rock face and came brawling down the broken slope, with no sign of a spring at all, let alone a green one.

Who was playing games? Loretta? The squaw?

Jokers like to watch their victims. He looked around carefully, angrily. As far as the eye could determine, he had this cliff and this creek to himself, and the whole world to boot.

He looked again at the cliff. Forty, fifty, some places sixty feet. Sharp, almost solid rock, with a few scrubs of jack pine clinging to cracks here and there, a spruce and hemlock at the foot. Up at the top, like as not, it would be flat earth soft as delta country—a giant terrace up to the mountain beyond.

Suddenly he saw an answer—the only possible way that the squaw could be right and Loretta not playing games. Not practical jokes, anyway.

He cast up and back along the face of the cliff until he located a possible break near the top—a long brown scar of spilled earth and the clinging evergreen thick around it. He rode to the foot of it, found shade for the pony, and started to climb a spruce which grew hard by the sheer wall. Near the treetop was a tangle of limbs, part from his tree, part from growth on the cliff. He thrashed his way across and began to crawl upward.

In twenty minutes he was winded and furious. He had been a fly, a mountain goat, a leapfrog, an inchworm. His fingernails were broken and there was dirt in his mouth and grit under his right eyelid. But the last fifteen feet or so were suddenly easy, with a dry wash he had not been able to see before, angling gently up to the right, and he got up it on his hands and knees, and at last reached level ground.

He didn't attempt to get to his feet at first, but stayed there on all fours with his head hanging, blowing like a foundered horse. When at last he raised his head, there was the spring, waiting for him.

It was not, strictly speaking, a spring. Here, too, water appeared out of a hillside. It ran only a hundred feet or so, then widened into a pool overhung by trees and thick bushes. The banks were shadowed and mossy, yet only a few feet away one could stand in the sun and look out over seventy miles of country. Uphill from the pool, the slope became steeper and ended in another, much more formidable cliff. The stream evidently was underground most of the way, and came stitching out just here, to make the pool and disappear again through some fissure in its bottom.

Scott pushed his way through the underbush to the edge of the water and stood a while, thinking nothing in the world but that this was a mighty nice place to be. Then he scanned the banks and the whole terrace and hillside with a mountain man's instinctive caution; and, seeing nobody, he took off his sweaty shirt and undershirt and doused them in the spring. He spread them on a flat rock to dry in the sun, then washed his head and neck and drank a little. Then he lay down in the mossy shade with his back against a boulder where he could see the whole pool with one flick of the eyes, and settled himself to wait.

He was, he realized with pleasure, early; by the sun, it couldn't be much past one o'clock. From the back pocket of his Levi's he extracted a small leather-bound book, and began to read.

"I never read a book in my life."

For the second time that day a disembodied voice spoke to him. Along with the flash of astonishment, and just as strong, was a surge of irritation. He bounced up and crouched, his eyes everywhere. That all they do between jobs, he thought angrily, make a monkey out of a man?

Then he saw her, and the anger faded, leaving only amazement. She stood in the split trunk of an Engelmann's spruce, her hatless head like a bright flower in the thick growth of mountain laurel which concealed the cleft. He crossed his big arms on his bare chest and said with an odd diffidence, "Beg pardon, ma'am; can't say I saw you there. Let me get my shirt."

She waded through the laurel and stepped out on the bank. "I've seen the like before," she said. "Don't put it on while it's wet. What were you readin'?"

"Cooper."

"What's a cooper?"

"It's a book called *Last of the Mohicans* by a man named Cooper."

"I never read a book in my life," she said again. She looked at the volume where it lay by the boulder, at Scott, at the book again. She seemed to be having a great deal of trouble getting used to the idea of a man reading a book. "What do you read books for?"

Now he laughed, and she flared up at him, "You laughing at me?"

"Lord, no, ma'am. It's just that nobody ever asked me that before." He looked at the still water for a moment, thinking. "Tell you what, suppose you had a friend, he knew a whole lot more than you do. He could tell you things about what people are like all over the world, the way they live, everything. And what folks were like a hundred years ago or even a thousand. He could tell you things that make your hair curl, lose you sleep, or things that make you laugh." He looked up at her swiftly, and away. "Or cry."

He kicked a pebble into the water and watched the sunlight break and break, and heal. "More than that. Suppose you had a friend there waiting for you anytime you wanted him, anyplace. He'd give you all he's got or any part of it, whenever you wanted it. And even more, you could shut him up if you didn't feel like listening. Or if he said something you like, you could get him to say it over a hundred times, and he'd never mind."

He pointed at the book. "And all that you can put in your pocket." Suddenly he faced her. "Talk a heap, don't I?"

"Yes," she said. But there was no objection in the word.

They stood by the water, their eyes trapped. Scott, then Loretta, tugged at the bond and for a moment couldn't break it. They were laughing embarrassedly, and laughing at their own laughter.

She sat down, and he went down beside her, close, but not too close. "How many books've you read?" she asked.

"Lord, I don't know."

"I'd know."

This time he did laugh at her. She looked up into his face without anger. They fell silent again, until he said, "Ma'am—"

"Don't call me that. Loretta's my name."

"Yes'm—Loretta. Thanks. Was going to say, I have two-three more books in my bunkroll, you like to read them." He waited a long time for her answer, but there was none. "What's the matter?"

"I guess," she said with difficulty, "I better not borrow a book."

He drew breath to ask her why not, but the strain in her voice warned him away. Something here . . . Conlin didn't like books, or didn't like her borrowing from the bunch . . . or maybe something which didn't concern Conlin at all. He could wait. It would come in time, if it was important. "Any time you change your mind," he said pleasantly.

She moved impatiently. "Don't you wonder why I asked you come up here?"

He shook his head.

A series of expressions chased themselves across her smooth face—puzzlement, anger, amusement. "I don't know whether to get mad at you for that," she said.

"You shouldn't."

"All right, why did I tell you to meet me?"

"You wanted somebody to talk to," he said immediately.

She made an odd sound, a short, surprised "Hm!" from her nostrils. Reluctantly her eyes met his. "What do you mean?"

"What I said. Someone to talk to," he said carefully. "All the time the same faces saying the same things—Conlin talking business, Al Coe bragging, and in between times," he added shrewdly, "trying on fancy clothes that nobody ever sees you in. Day after day . . . and you just naturally got to talk to someone."

"You see a lot!" she blurted, in a voice that should have been banter but came out real.

"I say something wrong?"

She thought about it, honestly searching. Then, "No. You have a way of . . . I don't know. I don't know how to say it, I'm just a . . . what I mean, it's hard to have secrets from you."

Wisely he said nothing.

"I'll tell you why I wouldn't borrow a book," she blurted. "You see, I don't read so good. If I tried to read one of your books I wouldn't know what the words meant, and you'd think I was ignorant, and that's why." She leaped to her feet.

"Sure you're ignorant," he said, and smiled up at her, watching her face pale and her nostrils arch. "You know what? I'm ignorant too. I can't run a printing press or play the vi'lin or tan a leather hide. You know things I don't know, you've been places I never heard of. Everybody's ignorant, Loretta, one way or another. Should I hold it against you you never happened to read books?"

"I never heard a man talk like you do," she breathed. "I never."

He rose at last, and went and got the book. "Here."

She hesitated, then took it. He said, "About the words, I'll get you a dictionary any time Conlin works a town big enough to find one in. Meanwhile you can write 'em down, or mark them right in the book, and ask me. Eight times out of ten I won't know what they mean either, but that's all right; sooner or later the dictionary'll straighten us out."

He turned away from her; it was kindness not to look at her face just then. He went to the flat rock and shook out his shirt. It was light and warm from the sun, dry and clean. He put it on and went back to her. She stood where he had left her, holding the book against her belt-buckle with both hands. He said, "You didn't climb no cliff to get here."

"No, no, I didn't," she said absently. "Come on, I'll show you how to get back an easier way."

"I have a pony down—"

"Come on."

They walked southward along the ledge, away from the shadowed pool and across a baking hell of broken rock. The terraced ground narrowed and tilted downward as they rounded the face of the mountain. Just before it turned into a rough trail there was an overhang, and in the shade the roan was tethered.

Loretta swung up on it before Scott could put out a hand to help her, and they continued down the trail. He glanced up at her occasionally; she rode in silence, evidently wrestling with some internal problem. The precipice at their left which was the one he had climbed, gradually became part of the sidehill, until at last it was fit for a two-legged animal to walk on. She reined in.

"You cut back here, angling down," she said. "You'll be under the bluff then. Just keep going till you get to your pony."

There seemed to be something else that needed saying, but neither could find words. He watched her until she vanished around the face of the mountain, then he watched where she had been. At length he sighed and turned back to find his pony and ride the creek-bed back to the hideout.

A hand on his shoulder, and up he came out of a shining dream of the New Mexican sun glaring off a page of Fenimore Cooper; but it wasn't print, it was a picture of a face with clear skin, hungry with puzzlement. But the thing was gone before he could grasp it. Then the hand touched him again. "Scott!"

He opened his eyes. Someone bent over him. "It's me, Conlin. Come on."

Scott slid into his pants and followed the smaller man through the firelit gloom of the bunkhouse and the false-backed cabin. He wished he could see Conlin's face.

Conlin led the way to a spot on the trail a short way from the cabin.

"This'll do," he grunted. "Siddown."

They sat on a rock in the shadows. Scott heard the faint scrape of Conlin's holster on the rock, and let himself yearn for his own Colt's.

"How'd you make out?" he asked.

Conlin ignored the question completely. "What did you do with yourself today?"

"Looked around."

"Where at?"

"Yonder."

"By yourself?"

"Mostly."

"All right," said Conlin, "I know you was with Loretta. I know why, too."

Scott remembered how quiet Conlin's voice was when something ugly was going on, like the time he'd walked into the poker game in the bunkhouse. He tried to remember if this quiet was different from Conlin's usual quiet, and he couldn't.

Conlin said, "It's all right. You passed."

"Passed?"

"Some men," said Conlin, "make it to the cliff and turn back. Some bull ahead the way you do and get to the spring. Some cast back and forth along the mountain until they find the easy way. Once one of 'em got lost doing that."

Scott listened, so utterly surprised that he ceased trying to make sense out of any of this.

"Those that get to the top are two kinds—the ones who make mistakes and the ones who don't. You didn't."

It seemed to be time for Scott to say something, so he asked, "You mean you set that up for me, all of it?"

"For you, for everybody. There's some hombres just got to make damn' fools of theirselves first chance they get, and the time to find it out is soon."

"Seems to me . . ." But Scott was learning fast. This was Conlin's method, Conlin's business.

"Spit it out, Scott."

"None of my business Jim."

"That's all right."

"All right then. Ain't you taking a long chance with Miss Loretta?"

Conlin laughed that quiet chuckle of his. "Not a partickle. First place, ninety-nine out of a hundred wouldn't chance tangling with me on the very first day here. Second place, Loretta can take care of herself. If she can't do it with the back of her hand, she'll do it with the derringer she carries. Third place, if anybody should move too fast or too rough for her, there's Henry Little Hawk on the second bluff, up over the spring, with a long bar'led Winchester and the damnedest eye I seen yet. I seen Henry split a bullet on a knife blade and put out two candles."

Half consciously Scott stroked his breastbone, imagining it suddenly slammed out between his shoulder blades before he could so much as hear the shot. He said, "You figure everything. And I don't know as I like that much, Conlin. I got to tell you that."

"You don't have to like it," said Conlin. "You didn't have to come here and you don't have to stay." The Bookkeeper paused, then said, "Here."

A small heavy cloth bag fell into Scott's slack hand. "All gold, four hundred dollars. Your half share for today."

Scott squeezed the bag and tossed it in his hand. Their shares—his and Conlin's—should come to $2400. The other shares—five if the breed got as much as the rest—brought it to $6400. He whistled.

"Sure you'll stay," said Conlin.

"Why not?"

Conlin chuckled. "Now, Scott, somethin' else. You might as well know right from the start that Loretta don't cotton to you much. You got too much book-learnin' and it scares her. But at the same time them books can be a godsend. She got a lot of time on her hands—I can't be keepin' her happy every single minute—and if you can get her to readin' books you'll be doin' her a favor and me too. Reckon you might loan her some book, somethin' easy to start on?"

I already did! thought Scott, with a vague start of excitement; this was coming through to him like a message from Loretta herself. He said, "If she'll take it."

"She won't at first," Conlin said positively, "but you just nip her along like a cow-dog till she's headed right."

"Can't promise," drawled Scott, "but I'll try."

There was a bang from the cabin—someone kicking open the false wall. "Right on schedule," said Conlin. "We all come back different ways, you know. They'll be driftin' in for the next hour. You go on back to your bunk. Next gold you get, you'll work for."

They got to their feet. "Come on, Henry," said Conlin. And as Scott's heart leaped into his throat, what looked like a rock shadow detached itself from the hillside and said, "Yup," and became Henry Little Hawk.

It was all Scott could do to start for the bunkhouse with an appearance of casualness. If Henry had been on that high bluff, he must have seen Scott give a book to the girl. Now Loretta was telling Conlin how reluctant she was. Was Conlin interested in exactly what lies were being told? Or would the fact of a lie be enough for a bullet out of the dark?

It wasn't until he was back in his bunk that he recaptured the picture of Loretta after he had handed her the book— Loretta pressing it close to her body.

That, he thought as he fell asleep again, is quite one hell of a woman.

The days sped by, easy to lose count of. Some of it was hard to take. On a ranch there's never enough time for all the work. At the hideout there was never enough work. The broken-down buildings, weathered almost to invisibility, had to stay the way they were. The horses could be cared for, shod, watered, fed, and exercised just so much. Conlin permitted a weird kind of poker, which started and finished with chips returned to their box and all tallies canceled out; it was about as satisfying as blowing the head off a glass of branch water. Target shooting and more than a very little game hunting were out; on a still day the shots would be heard for miles. Twice Conlin let men fight; they did it out in the open, starting when Conlin said they could and knocking off when he felt they'd popped off enough steam. It was all worth it, but it wasn't easy.

Most afternoons Scott would amble up to the house and he and Loretta would sit out on the front porch and bone over their books. They stayed in plain sight, without ever discussing the matter first. Sometimes they would sit silently for hours, saying nothing, until a character in Loretta's book "essayed" something or said something "uxorious," at which time she would yell for help.

Scott missed a dictionary; he was a reader, not a scholar, and many a turn of phrase that made sense to him in context were beyond explanation when he tried it word for word. But as the days went by, Loretta learned to hurdle the unfamiliar instead of running into it head on, and increasingly the books began to talk to her instead of fighting back.

Yet sometimes after a long silent period Scott would find himself looking into her eyes. This always made them laugh, and they learned to do it inwardly, without a sound and with barely a change of expression. And sometimes they would look out across the valley and see figures moving; if the figures happened to be Conlin and Henry Little Hawk, things seemed to get said that could come out at no other time; but if the Bookkeeper and his little shadow were out of sight, it was sensible to assume that one or the other was within hearing.

It was at one of these times, while Scott was peering down the valley to be sure the group of men he saw breaking a horse included Conlin and the breed, that he heard a slight and disturbing sound and turned quickly to see Loretta crying. He leaned forward and took her hand. "What's the matter?"

She took a long time to find the words, and they came out as if they were hard for her to use. "You," she said. "The way you treat me. You get up when I come in, you tip your hat. If I got something to say, you wait, just like you wait to let me through a door first. All that. It means . . ."

She had to tremble for a while, and then stop trembling. "Arch, don't you know where I come from, where Conlin found me, what I was doing, what I am? Sometimes I think you . . . don't know, and then I feel ashamed, the way you . . . And sometimes I think you do know, and all those things you do, they're making fun of me."

He kept his eye on the horses and let her have it out with herself. When she was quiet, he said, "Loretta, time was when I wasn't more housebroke than a four-week mongrel dog. I used to let my dinner run off my chin and I hadn't the wit to say whoa. Now am I the same Arch Scott? Sure I am. I grew up, that's all, and I don't do those things any more and never will again. Are you going to slap my hand today because I stuck it in a butter churn thirty years ago? Folks are what they are, not what they were."

"Arch," was all she said; but you couldn't write or say how it sounded; you couldn't paint a picture of how it looked.

There were other things said during these brief intervals of open speech between them. Things about past jobs Conlin had pulled, about the way he got his information. About the way he thought. And a good deal about his men. His complete, yet scornful reliance on Henry Little Hawk; how he trusted Big Ike Friend, and his thorough understanding of the Waley brothers, Moko and Gus, whom he had bought and who would sell out at any better offer. And of course, Al Coe.

Al Coe, the big, glittering, braided, pearl-inlaid two-gun-toter, was the only man there who had "failed" the Green Spring test. Conlin had known he would, and he himself had handled the Winchester. His single shot had clipped a boulder right by Coe's head, just the way a Kaintuck rifle-man barks a squirrel. He did it, he told Loretta, because he needed the man. He needed his noise and his color and the bragging, wheeling, roaring false front of him when they took a bank or robbed train passengers. The sight of him would strike terror into many a man who might take an even chance against anyone as small and ordinary-looking as Conlin, or such saddle tramps as the Waley brothers. And as Al Coe was only kind of front, for scaring people who were afraid of rattlesnakes, Big Ike Friend was another kind, for scaring people who are afraid of grizzly bears.

All this information came out in patches and drabs and small spurts of reminiscence. Scott never went after it openly, but he never forgot a word of it.

"Arch," Loretta murmured one afternoon as they leaned

together over a book freckled with her pencil marks, "you got to watch out. Al Coe's been to Jim about you."

"About you and me?"

"Yes, that's really why, but he wouldn't dare say so—Jim would kill him. Instead he's trying to make Jim suspicious of you. He says you're a railroad detective. He says he saw you seven years ago in New Mexico."

"Yellow," said Scott. "He ever make a play for you?"

"I told you. Only that once, at the spring."

"And he got his ears pinned back. That's what I mean, I tangled with him the day after I got here, and called him. Only that once. He's had nothing to say to me ever since. What'd Conlin say when Al told him that about New Mexico?"

"Told him to go dip his head in the trough. But—you never know what Jim is thinking."

"What do you think?"

She stepped back from the table and looked at him. "A man is what he is, not what he was," she said.

He grinned, his mouth dry.

Then one day Arch Scott went to town.

He went, of course, with Conlin's permission and blessing. Conlin was suspicious of men who didn't want an occasional ride to town; they built up pressures which were unpredictable if they should explode at the hideout, and Conlin liked to predict. Scott went by himself, after accepting Conlin's suggestion of company—Big Ike Friend; Conlin did not want Big Ike to go, but he did want to see how Scott would take the suggestion, and he was satisfied.

Afterward, Conlin got a full report on what Scott had done at Elwood—from Henry Little Hawk, of course. No, Scott had not seen Henry. The little man had squatted un-

der a blanket outside the rear door of the saloon while
Scott drank; he had been in a tree outside Flo Connery's
heavily curtained window during Scott's stop at Miz Flag-
ler's honkytonk. He had been sitting in the shadow of a
packing case across the street when Scott went into the general store and when Scott came out with the schoolmaster;
he had come up the alley by the school just in time to see
Scott accept a book from the schoolmaster and leave with it.

Scott had cooked and camped once on the way to Elwood, once on the way back. He had seen and spoken with
nobody, either time. Yes, Henry had had a word with Flo
Connery and with the bartender at the Last Chance Saloon.
Scott had been most discreet and had given no information.

Conlin received all this with satisfaction; he picked his
men the way he picked his jobs, with care and forethought.
He overlooked only one thing, and that simply because not
even Henry Little Hawk could be everywhere. He had no
inkling that two hours after Scott's departure the schoolmaster went to the sheriff's office with Scott's carefully
drafted map of Casson's Quarry, a neighboring mine and
cattle town, complete with the date and time and method
of Conlin's next raid.

Before sundown a deputy was on the stage road to Casson's Quarry, where, after some quiet discussion, a welcome
was secretly and efficiently prepared. They had more than a
week to sew up the details, there at Casson's Quarry, and
by the appointed day there were deputies and three sheriffs
and railroad men and bank men and even a United States
Marshal. Conlin was, indeed, in for a surprise, to discover
that a small army knew details possessed, he thought, only
by himself and the silent Henry Little Hawk.

And so, for a week after his return, life at the hideout proceeded in its quiet and uneventful way. Scott continued with his bookish visits to Loretta, who was pathetically grateful for the dictionary he brought back with him, and increasingly taken with the worlds, she read about—worlds of fashion, adventure, romance, scandal in high places.

She didn't have a chance to say goodbye to Scott. Without advance warning the whole gang, except for Henry Little Hawk who had gone on ahead, assembled two hours before sundown, saddled up, and rode. By the time they camped, most of them had a pretty shrewd idea as to where they were going; but nobody said anything about it until sunup, when they squatted around the fire with their black coffee and fatback and listened to Conlin.

"This here Casson's Quarry," Conlin said, squatting in front of a clean-swept place in the dust, "is hung on the side of a hill. Most of you been there so you know what it's like. I want you two who ain't seen it yet to listen even harder; there ain't nothin' clumsier than a man who thinks he knows everything."

He began to draw in the dust.

"This here's the main drag, they call the Stage Road. The town mostly tapers off gradual to the north and west, but here on the east there's a hogback that cuts it off real sharp. The Stage Road runs right down to that hogback, and the bank's spang on the last corner.

"Now, time was when the stage had to turn north a mile, on a road that angled up the hogback, and then switch back south to get down the other side, windin' up not forty yards away from the butt end of the main drag. Somebody got the idea of cuttin' through the hogback so the stage could drive straight through, so they done that, and it's their pride and joy; they opened it with speeches and all that, and everybody in town was drunk for two days.

"But if you go in town that way—and we do—you get through that cut and practic'ly fall into the bank. We don't scatter and we don't filter in, not this time; we go in together, fast and bunched up, and no yippin' an' ki-yi-in', either, hear me, Al? We take the bank and bounce back out again before anyone can so much as start for the sheriff's office—it's way the hell up the other end of the street.

"Coe, Ike, Scott—you three go in with me. Moko, you and your brother ride right past the front and down the alley at the other side and flush out anybody you see there. Go right around the back and around the bank to the front again and cover us—we ought to be out by then.

"Then we bunch up again and out we go through the cut. You all got it straight in your minds how to get back? Six of us—we go back six different ways. Just one thing—if you see Henry Little Hawk settin' on the hitchin' rail at the bank, go on by and don't even look at the place. We'll all go to the Piebald Bar and have a drink and go on home. Is there any questions?"

There were no questions. Conlin stood up and shuffled out the sketch he had made in the dust, and they mounted. They rode west for two miles and then left the trail and entered the woods. It was scramble and duck for a while, and once they had to lead their horses; but at last they emerged on the Stage Road, not a quarter of a mile from the cut.

From the middle of the road they could look through the hogback that barred the way like a high earthen wall, and straight up the main street of Casson's Quarry. It was all but deserted.

"Hey, Jim—bank open now, you reckon?"

"Sure, Ike. Cattle auction today, and payday at the mines."

"Don't see many people around."

"Let me do the worrying," said the Badlands Bookkeeper. "Let's get it done, boys."

They cantered down the road. They had it all to themselves.

Al Coe moved up beside Scott. "All the same to you, perfessor," he growled, "I'll stick by you."

Scott flicked a glance at him. It was the first time since that talk in the bunkhouse that Coe had said more to him than "Pass the salt."

"Help yourself, Coe," drawled Scott, "I ain't afraid to ride next to a target like that pretty hat."

"I don't figure they'll shoot no New Mexico lawman," said Coe.

"You and me," said Scott steadily, "we're going to settle this thing out, right quick."

"That's what I figure," said Coe, and he rode close.

"God," said one of the Waley brothers as they approached the cut, "a ghost town."

"Just early, that's all," said Ike.

"Let's go," said Conlin, and flicked his mount into a lope. They bunched, Al Coe shouldering Scott annoyingly. Scott glared at him, but then they were into the cut and too busy keeping out from under each other to argue.

And suddenly their way was blocked.

A small, tattered figure on a moldy gray mare suddenly appeared at the town end of the cut and ambled toward them. The little brown man seemed to be asleep on his mount.

"Chop 'im down," barked Big Ike to Conlin, who was in the lead.

"Chop hell, that's Henry!" Conlin tried to rein in, but for three, four seconds the idea didn't penetrate to the others and they crowded him at a dead run. "Whoa, dammit!" roared Conlin in the loudest voice Scott had ever heard from him.

They bumped and milled and cussed, and then all hell broke loose.

From the town end of the cut a dozen men appeared. From above, on each side, guns like thunder and lead like hail roared down. There must have been fifty men up there on the ridge, flat on their bellies, watching them come, and now half of them were pouring lead down into the ambush and half were diving and frog-hopping down the eastern slope, to close the trap at the other end.

"Back, get back!" shouted Conlin; but the last word was not a shout. It was an agonized grunt as a .44 slug tore through his thigh and into the side of his horse's neck. The horse screamed and reared, and Conlin fought back, twisting the animal around by brute strength, so that it was headed back through the cut as its forefeet touched the road.

Moko Waley and his mount were down, kicking and spitting their lives out; Conlin jumped them. His horse screamed again as he lunged forward.

There was a confused motion in front of him—Big Ike leading him pace for pace for an interminable moment; Big Ike, the only one of his crew who'd stick by him, stick for sure, no matter what—then Big Ike throwing his guns up in the air, riding with his hands up and empty, and terror on

his face as he swung his head from side to side, hoping someone in the posse would see him surrendering.

To one side was Gus Waley, afoot, hands up too. On the
other side was Al Coe, maybe in a panic, crowding Arch
Scott to a standstill against the rock wall.

Then there was nothing ahead of Conlin but a line of
men across the road, between him and the badlands, and
suddenly he was afloat in the air, his horse gone out from
under; and then a jarring, red-hazed impact as he fell, and
the wound in his thigh scalding with road grit. He got one
foot up, the other knee under him, and wavered there; then
there was a thunder of hoofs behind him and Henry Little
Hawk landed lightly in the dust. The little breed caught
Conlin under the armpits and heaved. It was a desperate,
impossible effort; Conlin threw out an arm for balance and
felt his hand on a saddle horn.

Then somehow he was lying face down on the back of
the breed's gray mare, rushing the line of deputies, riding
two of them down.

When Conlin glanced back, he saw Henry Little Hawk
lying in the road, one leg twisted crazily. He was propped
up on his elbow, waving goodbye like an old woman watching a train pull out of a depot.

There were horsemen at the town end of the cut, but none
here; and the cut was full of crazy horses, dead horses, dead
and crazy men; so Conlin got clean away on the breed's
horse.

Back in the cut Arch Scott was crowded to the wall by
Coe and his big black stallion. A man afoot, with a big shiny
star pinned to his vest, shouted, "This way, Mr. Scott, this
way, I'll cover you."

A hurt-animal sound woke her, and she lay dazedly for a moment, thinking it was part of some unhappy dream. But then she heard it again and flew out of bed and down the narrow stairs.

Out front, on the grass near the door, Jim Conlin lay face down making the noise. A few feet away stood Henry's gray mare, blown and foundered, the reins over her head and a rope of spittle carrying clear from her bloody mouth to the ground.

Loretta got the Bookkeeper inside somehow, and somehow got his clothes off and washed away that special mud made of dust, blood, and sweat, until she could find out where he was hurt. Actually it wasn't much of a wound, as such things go—a little hole here and a large one nearby where the slug had gone through. It had missed the thigh-bone and had almost stopped bleeding. But it hurt, and maybe it wouldn't heal. She did what she could. She did pretty well.

He didn't talk for a long time. When he did, he said, "All gone. All, all gone. He saved me, Loretta, and he died."

"Big Ike?"

"Big Ike!" he snorted. "Tucked his tail down and threw away his guns."

"Al Coe?"

"Dead. They shot him dead, then they shot him some more."

She had to know, but . . . don't ask, don't ask; maybe—"The Waleys?"

"Moko dead. Gus, he and Big Ike quit." Conlin half rose, screwing up his face. "Big Ike surrendered, you know that?" he shouted.

"Shh. Shh. Did . . . was it Arch Scott who saved you?"

"Damn it, I told you." He sank back. "I always said 'the breed.' Never slept in the bunkhouse with the others. He never asked to, but I tell you, I'd have laughed if he ever did, kicked his butt, the breed. Never ate with us white men, except campin'. He was the one, the only damn one—he saved me, and he died."

"Henry," she identified finally.

"All eyes, all brains. Tried to warn us, then he saved me, then he died."

She hit herself softly on the temples. "Jimmy, for the love of God—"

"All gone. That Coe, crazy as hell. Never tried to fight, never tried to run. Hung on to Scott, watching him every second, then shot him in the head. Then they cut Coe to pieces—crazy . . ."

"Scott—dead?"

"All gone," said the Bookkeeper. "All gone."

After a time he said, "Loretta?"

"Get some sleep," she said hoarsely. "You got to get some sleep."

He nodded weakly. "Yuh. Some . . . Loretta, they'll be comin'. Big Ike, if he'd quit, he'd bring 'em. And Gus Waley. Always said he'd sell me out for a good enough price. They got the price now—his dirty neck for mine." He breathed painfully for a while. "We'll take all the gold we can carry, Loretta. You pack anything you want, and we'll start again some place." He caught up with his breathing again, then opened his eyes and looked around the lamplit room. "Loretta?"

But she was not there.

In the morning Jim Conlin woke up. He had a fever. There was a bottle of water nearby and he drank it all.

There was also a note

i didn't take nothing but my dictionary i'm going in the morning if you can understand that then i'm going back to work don't try and find me not ever.

L.

"All, all gone," Conlin muttered. He dragged himself upstairs and got fresh clothes. He wondered what had happened. Al Coe had said Scott was a railroad man, but Al was always a trouble-maker. Henry, he'd know what happened.

He found Henry's long Winchester. It made a pretty good crutch. He got to his cache and took as much gold as he could drag. It wasn't much. He inched it down to the corral and caught a gelding and got the gold on. He roped a black, an old one, but the only one that would hold still for the kind of roping he was doing now. He got a saddle on it, led it to the bars, and climbed up on them and fell into the saddle. He rode off, leading the gelding.

They found the gelding, dead, in a ravine a month later. They got that gold and all that was in the cache too. Jim Conlin, the Badlands Bookkeeper, was never caught. Maybe the Mexicans got him, maybe fever. Maybe he's still alive.

Ride In, Ride Out

THEODORE STURGEON and DON WARD

> *Beware the fury of a patient man.*
> —From the Chinese

Midafternoon and he came to a fork in the road, just like the rest of us in all our afternoons, whether we know it at the time or not.

Younger Macleish liked the left fork. His horse's sleepy feet preferred the right, a bit downgrade as it was, and Macleish thought what the hell, he was ready to like the right fork too. He liked the country right, left, and whatever, from the white peaks feeding snow water to high timber and good grama range, across and down through the foothills where the low curly bunch-grass grew, and on to the black-earthed bottomland. But then it didn't need to be all that good to please Younger Macleish today. He was of a mind to like salt-flat or sage, crows, cactus or a poison spring, long as the bones lay pretty there.

Around the mountain (right fork, left fork, it's all the same) and three hundred miles beyond lay fifteen thousand well-fenced acres and a good warm welcome. Ninety-nine times Younger Macleish had said no to his cousin's offer, for he had some distances to pace off and some growing up to do on his own. Now he'd said yes and was ambling home to a bubbling spring and an upland house; not too far away lived a pair of the prettiest blue-eyed sisters since crinolines were invented, while down the other way—if a man found he couldn't choose—lived an Eastern school-marm with a bright white smile and freckles on her nose. Right now he had four months pay in his poke, his health, a sound horse, a good saddle and no worriments. If a man likes where he's been and where he's headed, he's fair bound to like where he is.

As the shadows grew longer, this horse, he thought ap-provingly, has the right idea, for the trail is good and the passes this side of the mountain might make a little more sense after all. And if things are as they should be, there'll be a settlement down yonder, maybe big enough for a hotel with a sheet on the bed and a bite of something other than trail bacon and boiled beans.

With the thought came the settlement, opening up to him as the trail rounded a bluff. It was just what he had in mind, plus a cut extra—a well-seasoned cowtown with a sprin-kling of mining. It had two hotels, he saw as he rode in, the near one with a restaurant and a livery right handy to it. There was a mercantile, more cow than plow, and half the barber shop was an assay office.

Younger Macleish rode up to the livery and slid off. He hooked an elbow around the horn and arched his back hard.

"Ridin' long?"

Macleish turned around and grinned at the tubby little old baldhead who stood in the carriage door. "My back says so . . . Treat hosses po'ly here, do you?"

The old man grinned in return and took the bridle. "Misable," he asserted. "Whup 'em every hour."

"Well, whack this'n with a oat or two an' give him water if he wants it or not."

"He'll rue the day," said the oldster, his eyes twinkling.

Macleish followed him far enough inside for a glance to assure him that water really was there and that the hay was hay. Then he unbuckled his saddlebags and heaved them over his shoulder. "Which one o' them hotels is best?"

"One of 'em ain't rightly a hotel."

"I'll start out at the other."

"The near one, then. Miz Appleton, now, she *feeds*." The old man colored his information by casting his eyes upward most devoutly.

"Now, you know I ain't et since my last meal?" Chuckling, Younger Macleish humped his saddlebags and stepped out into the street. It was only a step to the hotel porch, barely time enough to say howdy twice to passers-by. Macleish mounted the steps and thudded inside. It was small in there, but it had a stairway with a landing up the left and across the back, and under the landing, just like in the city but littler, a regular hotel kind of desk. He knew something was cooking right now, somewhere in the place, with onions and butter both, and he knew that not long ago something had been baked with vanilla in it. Everything was so clean he wanted to go out and shine his boots and come in again. Behind the desk was a doorway covered by nothing at all but red and blue beads. These moved and fell to again behind a little lady fat as the old livery man, but half his age and not the least bit bald. Her face was soft and plump as a sofa pillow and she had a regular homecoming smile.

"You'll be Miz Appleton."

"Come in. Put down those bags. You've come a ways, the looks of you. You hungry?"

Macleish looked around him, at the snowy antimacassars and the doilies under the vases of dried ferns and bright paper flowers, all of it spotless. "I feel dirtier'n I do hongry, but if I git any hongrier I'll be dead of it. My name's Younger Macleish."

"You hurry and wash," she ordered him like kinfolk, "while I set another something on the stove. You'll find water and soap on the stand in your room, first right at the head of the stairs." She gave him a glad smile and was gone through the wall of beads before he could grin back.

He shouldered his saddlebags and climbed the stairs, finding the room just where she had said, and just what the immaculate downstairs had led him to expect. He stood a moment in it shyly, feeling that a quick move would coat the walls with his personal grime, then shrugged off the feeling and turned to the washstand.

He had no plan to get all that fancied up; he just wanted to be clean. But clean or not, just plain shirtsleeves didn't feel right to him in that place, and all he had to put over it was his Santiago vest. It had on it some gold-braid curlicues and a couple extra pockets and real wild satin lapels that a puncher might call Divin' W if it was a brand. He put it on after he'd shaved till it hurt and reamed out his ears; he had half an idea Miz Appleton would send him back upstairs if they weren't clean. He took off his pants and whacked off what dust he could, and put them on again and did his best to prettify the boots. When he was done he cleaned up from his cleaning up, setting the saddlebags in a corner and folding away his dirty shirt. He hung up his gunbelt, never giving it a second thought, or much of the first one either, bent to look in the mirror and paste down a lock of hair which sprang up again like a willow sapling, and went downstairs.

Miz Appleton clasped her hands together and cried out when she saw him: "Glo-ry! Don't he look nice!" and Younger Macleish looked behind him and all around to see who she was talking about, until he saw there was no one there but himself and the lady. "It ain't me, honest, ma'am," he said. "It's only this here gold braid."

"Nonsense! You're a fine-looking, clean-cut youngster. Wherever did you get that curly hair?"

He felt his ears get hot. He never had figured an answer to that. Women were always asking him that. Next thing you know she'd be saying he'd ought to be an actor. But she was asking him if he was ready to eat. He grinned his answer and she led him through a door at the end of the little lobby into the restaurant.

The restaurant had a door also into the street, which Macleish thought was pretty clever. It was a rectangular room, just big enough for three square tables and one long one. On each was a bowl of the dried flowers he had seen in the lobby. The big table had two of them. The whole place smelled like Sunday supper in the promised land. At one of the tables, two punchers and a man in a black coat were shoveling away silently as if the promise was being kept.

Along the back wall was a doorway covered with the same kind of bead curtain. Through it he could just barely make out another table, smaller than the others, covered with blinding white linen. He saw glasses there and a silver vase and a silver candlestick that matched it.

"Just you set," said Miz Appleton, waving at one of the bare square tables, "and I'll be right with you."

Macleish said, "Real nice place here." He pointed at the bead-screened alcove. "Who's that for?"

"You want to see it?" Proudly beaming, she went to the alcove, took a wooden match from a box in her apron pocket, leaned in and lit the candle in the silver candlestick.

"Well, hey," breathed Younger Macleish.

The alcove was just big enough for two people and the table. The seats were built right on to the wall like a window box. They had velour cushions and backs on them. Two places were set. At each place were three forks, two knives, four spoons, three glasses, and a starched napkin folded in a circle like a king's crown, with the eight points sticking straight up. The cutlery looked all mismatched, but the handles were all the same: wide fork, narrow fork, thin knife, wide knife. The same with the glasses, all different shapes but with identical bases. He had never seen anything like it.

He asked again, "Who's this for?"

"Anyone who likes to eat this way."

"Now who would that be?" asked Macleish, honestly perplexed.

"I might say anyone who knows the difference between eating and dining." She laughed at him suddenly. He was walleyed as a new calf seeing his first bull. "Or anybody that might like to learn."

He wet his lips. "Me?"

She laughed at him again. "You're right welcome, Mr. Macleish." Then, in tones of real apology, "It's got to cost a little more, though, and take a while to fix."

"Oh that's all right," he said quickly, his eyes on the

gleaming table. He picked up a salad fork between his fingertips and carefully set it down again. "You're goin' to have to break trail for me through all this."

She laughed again and told him to set right down. She seemed to think he was no end funny, and he imagined he was; but there's ways and ways of getting laughed at, and he didn't mind her way. He sat down, careful not to bump anything, and she whisked away the second place setting and left with it.

She was back in a moment with a dish, a long narrow oval of cut glass in which were arranged six celery stalks and a mound of what looked like olives only they were shiny black. She set it down and gently removed the napkin from under his chin and spread it on his lap, while he sat rigidly with his big scrubbed hard-work hands hidden under the edge of the table. "I 'spect some folks think I'm addled in the head," she chattered, "but I always say that good manners are the only real difference between the men and the beasts. I don't reckon there's another table like this this side of San Diego, not till you reach St. Louis. Don't just stare at those olives, boy—eat 'em! . . . It just does me good to have someone *dine* instead of feed. Or learn it," she added quickly and kindly. "Here." And from under her arm she took a great big card and laid it before him.

MENU, it announced itself in block type at the top. All the rest was in script—flowery curly Spencerian script, so neat and straight and pretty that he just wagged his head in amazement over it. He could make out every single letter —but not one of the words.

"It's in French," she explained. "All real high-toned menus in real high-toned places are written in French. This one's from the Hotel Metropole in San Francisco. I had my

honeymoon there with Mister Appleton." She smiled a little
more brightly, even, than usual, and Macleish had the vague
feeling that something hurt her. "I put that menu away and
kep' it for twelve years, and I said to myself that someday
I'd serve up that dinner again in a place of my own, and
now I do. These," she explained, "are the appetizers, and
this is the soup. Down here is fish and then meat. Here
and here are vegetables and potatoes and all that, and then
dessert and so on."

"Appetizers?"

"They hone up your appetite. Make you hungry."

He wagged his head again at the idea of folks needing to
be made hungry at dinnertime. He squinted at the card
and said, "Chat. Chat."

"Chateaubriand," she read out. "You cook beef in wine."

"Why?"

She laughed. "Ask yourself that when you've tasted it."

He forlornly handed her back the card. "I better leave
all this to you, Miz Appleton. You just bring it on and tell
me what to do."

She left him munching on a stalk of celery. Each stick
was packed full of a gooey, blue-y stuff that tasted like
cheese and, as Miz Appleton explained to him when she
came back to pour him a glass of very dry sherry, *was*
cheese. He inhaled the whole dishful and drank the wine
at a gulp, and sat there with his stomach growling for more.

So Younger Macleish ate a fragrant thin soup with crisp
tiny fried cubes of bread afloat in it, some tender flakes of
trout meat, four popovers, five salted breadsticks and two
rolls; another dish of stuffed celery and olives, three helpings of the chateaubriand and all the fixings that went with
it; and four pieces of lemon meringue pie you could have

sneezed off the plate it was so light. He drank white wine and red wine, sharp and thin, and at the end, in a third glass, a heavy red port that his tongue roots couldn't believe. Nuts came with this, and a silver thing to crack them with, and a little bitty doll's house sort of cup of coffee. Somewhere along the line he had lost the conviction that genteel folk didn't know anything about eating, the helpings seemed so small; because they kept coming and coming, until at last he had to sneak a quick pull on his cinches and let his belt out a notch, silently commanding his liver to move over and make more room. Packed with well being until it showed on his face in a sheen of sweat, he pressed limply at a nut in the nutcracker and wondered if Mr. Appleton was still alive or had died happy of eating.

"Mr. Appleton was killed on the way back," said the little lady when she brought more coffee, smiling that brighter-than-usual smile. "The trace chain broke. He threw me clear but he went over with the horses. The only thing I can't give you," she went on rapidly, "is a brandy. At the Metropole you'll see the gentlemen sitting around after their dinner smoking their fine Havana see-gars, and there'll be brandy, just a little drop of it in the bottom of a big glass like a flower vase. That's so they can smell it better. Or sometimes they'll call for a shot-glass too and pour in a little brandy and dip the end of their see-gar into it. Or put a drop or two right into their coffee. I do wish I had a bit of fine old brandy for you, so you'd know how it is. They always used to call for the oldest brandy, because that's best."

Killed on the way back, Macleish silently repeated to himself. That would be from a honeymoon. He said, "It's all right about the brandy, Miz Appleton. I doubt I'd git a drop of anything all the way down. Not till tomorrow noon or so anyhow."

"Well, I wish you had it all the same. How do you feel?"

"Miz Appleton," he said with all his heart, "I ain't lived such a life that I deserved all this."

"I think you have," she told him. "I think you will. You're a nice young man, Mr. Macleish."

He felt his ears getting hot again and stood up and batted his way through the red and blue beads and got clear of the alcove. Either he had to escape from all this goodness or he had to take a walk and shake down this dinner so he'd be able to lie down without spilling. He thanked her again and left her beaming after him, with her quick small hands folded together under her apron.

He'd already been past the livery and the mercantile, so he naturally ambled the other way. The town had its quota of bars, and a school right in town, and a church. Then there was a bank and a long row of dwellings and what do you know, a second mercantile, this one with a feed and grain warehouse attached. Then a smithy, and then the other hotel which, as the livery man had told him, wasn't rightly a hotel. He passed the entrance with a glance over the batwings, went on three paces and then stopped.

It wasn't the off-voice piano that stopped him, nor the size of the place, which was considerable for such a town, nor the glimpse of pink satin and soft hair somewhere along the bar, nor even the bar itself, the longest and most elaborate he had ever seen. It was the array behind the bar—four tiers all of twenty feet long each, rows and rows of bottles of all sizes and shapes. He had to wonder if there wasn't a fine old brandy there. He didn't want it or need it, and he didn't know if he'd like it or not, but Miz Appleton had said he ought to have it. It was like a service to her. The dinner seemed to mean more to her even than it had to him, and it just seemed right to finish it off the way she said.

So he turned back and went into the place.

The bartender was a squint-eyed oldster wrapped in a long white butcher's apron. You had an idea who he was talking to when you were by yourself at the bar, but it must have been pretty mystifying when the place was crowded. "You got any brandy?" Macleish asked.

One of the man's eyes scanned Younger Macleish's fancy vest while the other one raked the northwest corner. "Reckon we have."

"Real old brandy?"

"It's old."

"You got see-gars?"

"Two kinds. Most men wouldn't smoke the one, an' most men wouldn't pay for the other."

"Gimme the best," said Younger Macleish. He remembered something else and said "Uh," as the bartender was about to turn away. He couldn't see himself asking for a flower vase to drink his brandy out of, so he asked for the other instead. "Bring me a extra shot-glass with the brandy."

The bartender walked to the far end and got an old kitchen chair with the back off it, and carried it back and set it down. Grunting, he got up on it and reached for a bottle on the fourth tier. He brought it down and held it so Macleish could see the label, but didn't set it down and didn't bring glasses. "Suit you?"

The question was asked in a way that seemed to mean more than it said. Macleish wondered if it had anything to do with money. He noticed suddenly that the girl, the one

with the pink satin dress and all that hair, was watching
him. He went into his poke and got a gold ten dollars and
laid it on the wood. "It'll do," he said as if he knew what he
was talking about.

The bartender put the bottle down then and pulled the
cork, and reached underneath for a glass with a small stem
and a big bell, and the extra shot-glass. Macleish figured
that if you drink brandy out of a big glass like that it must
be something like beer; but when the bartender poured in
only about a finger and quit, he remembered what Miz
Appleton had said about the men smelling it. He took it
and smelled it while the bartender went for the cigars. It
smelled fine.

The bartender brought the cigar box and handed the
whole thing to him, and he took out three. Two he stuck
in his vest and got the other one going. The smoke was full-
fleshed and kind to him. He took a little taste of the brandy
and waited a second, and it was as if a good spirit had sat
down in his throat in velvet pants. Turning his back to the
bar and hooking up his elbows, he began a wordless
worship of Miz Appleton and all her works. He was vaguely
aware that the bartender was leaning across the far end,
talking to the girl in pink, that the piano player expressed
his disbelief in his own abilities by working with his fingers
crossed, and that two faro games were operating in the
corner. But none of this mattered to him; and as he swung
around to dunk his cigar in the shot-glass and caught
the pink girl's eye as she climbed the stairs to the gallery,
the moment of self-consciousness was lost in pure joy when
he took his first drag of the brandied smoke.

He stood in this golden trance for some minutes and nobody bothered him until the girl came back downstairs and

walked over to him. He smiled at her because he was ready to smile at anything, but if it was the first word she waited for, she'd have to give it; he couldn't think of a one.

"Hello," she said.

Well, that was a good one. He gave it right back to her.

"Stranger here, aren't you?" She was older than he had first thought, but not much. She had a real different kind of nose, thin as the back of a knife between her close-set eyes, and flaring out at the nostrils, which pointed more forward than down and were constantly aquiver. She was pretty enough, though, with all that hair. He admitted that he was a stranger, and took another smell of the brandy because he then and there ran out of anything else to say.

"Come to stay?" she asked him.

"Nope," said Younger Macleish.

"That's too bad," said the girl, and then laughed briefly and loudly. "My," she said, "you're quite a one for talk, aren't you? . . . You going to buy me a drink?"

"Oh!" said Macleish, feeling stupid. "Uh—sure."

She nodded over his shoulder and the bartender brought her a pale something in a small glass. He also brought back change from Macleish's money. He didn't bring much.

"What are you going to do with yourself all evening?"

"Look around," said Macleish uncomfortably.

It seemed to him that she waited altogether too long to say anything else, watching him the whole time. The bartender was watching him too, or her; he wouldn't know. At last she burrowed into a pink beaded bag and withdrew a heavy gold compact. "Look here," she said, and opened the lid. Macleish became aware of a faint tinkling. He leaned close and discovered that in shrill small bell-like notes, the compact was playing "Peas, peas, goober peas."

"Well, hey," said Younger Macleish.

"I got more of them," said the girl. "I got a powder box that plays a waltz and another one—that one's only a straight music box—that plays the Trish-Trash Polka."

"You *do?*" said Macleish, sounding quite as impressed as he was.

"You want to see 'em? I got them upstairs."

He looked at her numbly. In his mind he had a swift flash of two crinolined sisters and a white-smiled schoolmarm, and—and the whole idea of going home to settle. Then there was this girl and what she said, it . . . it . . . Well, somehow, something was altogether mismatched.

"I guess I better not," he mumbled.

"Oh—come *on!*" she said; and then, going all tight-lipped, "It's just to see the music boxes. What do you think I *am?*"

He knew his ears were getting red again; he could feel the heat. He wished he could get out of this. He wished he hadn't come in. He wished he could curl up in his cigar-ash and go up in smoke. He said, "Well, all right."

He drank up his brandy and it stung him harder than he wanted it to. He dipped his cigar once more in the shot-glass and followed her up the stairs. He was dead certain that both faro games must have stopped dead while he climbed, everyone watching, but when he flashed a glance from the top everything down there seemed as usual. It was about then he remembered to breathe again. He turned to follow the girl along the gallery.

She had opened a door and was waiting for him. "In here."

It was black dark in there. If he thought anything at all, it was that she would follow him and light a lamp.

The instant he was clear of the door, it was kicked shut

with the girl still outside, and he found himself in total
blackness. Hands came from nowhere, took both arms,
wrenched them behind him. "Whut—" he yelled, and got a
stinging blow in the mouth before he could make another
syllable. He kicked out and back as hard as he could, and
his heel struck what felt like a shin-bone. He heard a curse,
and the red lightning struck him twice more on the cheek
and on the ear.

He stood still then, head down, hauling uselessly at the
relentless grip on his arms, and breathed hoarsely.

A blaze of light appeared across the room. It was only a
match, but it was so unexpected it hurt him more than fists
and made him grunt. The flare dwindled as it stroked the
wick of a lamp, and then the lamp-flame came up, yellow
and steady.

The room was fixed up like an office. There was a book-
case and a cabinet and, on the wall, a claims map. A big
desk stood parallel with the far wall with a heavily curtained
window behind it. The lamp stood on the desk, and seated
behind it was a thin man with pale gray hair and the bright-
est blue eyes he had seen yet. The man wore a black coat
and a tight white collar and an oversized black Ascot, from
the top bulge of which gleamed a single pearl. The man
was waving the match slowly back and forth to put it out.
He was smiling. His teeth were very long, especially the eye-
teeth.

"So, Mr. Bronzeau," he said in a soft, mellow voice. "We
meet at last."

Younger Macleish was far too dazzled to respond. He
pulled suddenly at the arms which held him, glanced right
and left. He got a blurred picture of one man, heavy-set and
running to fat, who smelled of beer and sweat, and another,

much younger, with the crazed, craven face of one who can be frightened into being snake-dangerous. One thing was certain: the two of them knew how to hold a man so he couldn't move. To them he said, "Turn me loose."

At this there was a movement in the shadows and a fourth man moved out of the corner. He was a wide man with a wide hat on, and small eyes, and he put two big white hands in the pool of light under the lamp and began to fiddle with a big black and gold signet ring with a black-letter B on it. He was smiling. Younger Macleish said again, "Turn me loose."

"Oh," said the gray-headed man pleasantly, "we will— we will, Mr. Bronzeau. But first Mr. Brannegan here will relieve you of anything sharp or explosive or which in any way might disturb the peace and quiet of our little conversation." He smiled, and then waved his hand in a small flourish at the man with the signet ring. He said, like one politician introducing another politician, "Mr. Brannegan."

The big man came over. Macleish tensed. "Hold real still, sonny," said Brannegan, and went over Macleish rapidly and with an expert touch. He checked everything—even his boot-tops, where men have been known to stash a knife. In the process he got Younger Macleish's money, his cigars, his matches and even a walnut he had borrowed from Miz Appleton's alcove. These things he put neatly on the desk.

"I shall now show you, Mr. Brannegan, that even you can at times be careless; and you, Mr. Bronzeau, that I know a great deal more about you than you thought I did. Our young friend," he informed Brannegan, "has been seen to reach up as if to scratch his ear, and suddenly hang a weighted throwing knife he carries in a four-by-four thirty yards away. If you will be good enough to look, I think you will find the knife in a sheath between his shoulder blades."

Brannegan swore and reached over Macleish's shoulder, to pound him heavily on the back. The two men holding him tightened their grip as Brannegan grasped Macleish's collar and with one painful wrench broke his string tie and tore out his collar buttons. He slid a hand down the back of Macleish's neck and scrabbled around as if he expected to find the weapon under the skin rather than on it.

"It ain't here," said Brannegan.

For a split second the gray-headed man's eyes got round; then they slitted again and he took to wagging his head sadly, side to side. "You have surprised me," he said to Macleish, "Mr. Bronzeau, you have indeed surprised me, and I concede that I never thought you would. I knew you would follow me here, and I knew you could be induced to come into this room; but I will allow that I never expected you to come unarmed. There is a difference, Mr. Bronzeau, between courage and foolhardiness. I think you will agree that you have passed it. Well then," he barked in a business-like way, "we can settle our little matter all the better, then." He took a paper out of his breast pocket, unfolded it and put it on the desk. "Here, my young friend, is a transfer form, properly executed, lacking only your signature. "Here," he said, moving an inkwell and a feather pen next to the paper, "is something to—"

"Now you looky here," said Younger Macleish, who had suddenly had enough and to spare, and was able to pull his startled wits back into shape. "I don't know you or nothing about you or no paper. Now turn me loose!" he yelled at the two men at his sides, and gave a mighty wrench that ought

to be enough to pull a horse off its feet—and wasn't enough
to break free of these two.

"Mis-ter Bronzeau!" cried the gray-headed man. He
sounded aggrieved—astonished and hurt. "You interrupted
me!" He turned to Brannegan, complaining: "Mister Brannegan, he interrupted me."

Brannegan tsk-tsked like a deacon, settled his big ring
just the way he wanted, and hit Macleish on the left cheekbone with it. Then he stepped back and smiled. He said,
"You hadn't ought to interrupt, sonny."

The craze-frightened youth snickered. The beer-smelling
man brayed. The gray-headed man waited until it was quiet
again except for Macleish's heavy breathing. The blood began running from the place the ring had hit.

"First I talk," the gray-headed man explained patiently,
"and then you talk, and that's the way gentlemen conduct
business. Now then—where were we? Here is a paper, and
here is the pen you are going to use to sign it with, and here
is something"—he put out a short-handled, long-bladed
knife, picked up the matchstick he had used to light the
lamp, and delicately split it in two—"we can use to keep this
conversation going if we have to; and here," he said as he
put the knife down exactly parallel with the pen and opened
the desk drawer, "is a little something for dessert, you might
say," and next to the knife he put down a nickel-plated, four-
barrel gambler's gun. "Just a toy, really, and guaranteed not
to hit what you aim at unless," he added, picking up the gun
and pointing it playfully at Macleish's belt-buckle, "you've
got some way of holding the target still." He laughed
genteelly; Brannegan haw-hawed; and late, the youth tittered and the beery man brayed. "Now then," said the gray-

headed man, "Mr. Bronzeau had something to say. Go ahead, Mr. Bronzeau."

Younger Macleish looked from one to the other of them and concluded that they were waiting for him to speak. He said, "My name ain't Bronzeau or whatever it was you said. I just rode in an' I'm goin' to ride out in the morning and you got yourselves the wrong man."

"Ah," said the gray-headed man tiredly, "come off it, Bronzeau. We know you. Don't make this take any longer than it has to."

"It's the truth all the same," said Younger Macleish.

"All right, all right; I'll hear it out. Where is it you pretend to be coming from, and what lie have you got ready about where you're going?"

"That," said Macleish, "is my business."

"He's rude, Mr. Brannegan," complained the gray-headed man.

Brannegan hit Macleish on the same place with his ring. It seemed to grow dark in there for a time, or perhaps it was only that the lamp and the room and all the men moved far off for a moment. Then he straightened up and shook his head, and it all came back again, and Brannegan was rubbing his ring and saying, "Don't be rude, sonny."

"Are you going to sign it?"

"No, I ain't."

"Not quite so hard this time, Mr. Brannegan." But Macleish guessed Brannegan did not hear the gray-headed man in time.

The next question he was aware of hearing was "Why? Why? Why put yourself through this, Mr. Bronzeau? Why won't you sign it? Just tell me that."

"Because I told you," said Macleish hoarsely. "I ain't who

you think, and this has nothin' to do with me. Now you whoa!" he roared suddenly at Brannegan, who was cocking his signet hand for another pass; and, surprisingly, Brannegan whoaed. Macleish said, "Whatever that is, it won't be worth nothing if I sign it. You might's well sign it yourself. I tell you it's got nothin' to do with me."

"Reasonable, reasonable," nodded the gray-headed man. "Only we just don't believe you." But Macleish noticed he didn't call him "Mr. Bronzeau" this time.

Brannegan said to the gray-headed man, "He ought to've had that there throwin' knife."

"A point, a point," allowed the gray-headed man, who apparently always repeated himself when he was thinking. "What impresses me most is that our Mr. Bronzeau is too intelligent to carry this performance of injured innocence on so long. Ergo, this man is as stupid as he acts. Which would indicate that he is after all not our Mr. Bronzeau." He pulled his low lip carefully away from his lower teeth. They were too long too. "On the other hand, such stupidity might be covering up a very clever man indeed. Indeed." Abruptly he turned from his contemplation of Younger Macleish and said briskly, "Mr. Brannegan, we need to know a little more about our young friend."

Brannegan said to Macleish, "Where at's your horse?"

Macleish said, "In my hip pocket."

"Sonny," said the big man, stroking his ring, "I owe you one for that."

"Take care of it when you come back," said the gray-headed man. "I'm sure all he meant was that his horse is at the livery, and would hardly be anywhere else."

"That's right," said Macleish.

Brannegan went to the door. The gray-headed man said,

"If by any chance this is not our Mr. Bronzeau, Brannegan, I should like to know it quickly. I tire soon in the presence of stupid people," and he smiled at Macleish.

"Be right back," said Brannegan, and went out.

The gray-headed man picked up the little gambler's gun and checked the load. "You may as well sit down and be comfortable," he said, waving at a corner chair. "Turn him loose, boys," he said, mimicking Macleish's earlier demand, "and stand by the door, and if he makes a play," he added, smiling his most pleasant smile, "kill him."

The men let go, and Macleish gave each of them a memorizing kind of look, and went and sat in the corner, folding his arms and massaging his biceps.

It grew very quiet in there. Macleish looked at the three, and the three looked back at him. After a while, the gray-headed man rose and came around to the front of the desk, holding the gun loosely. He stood back against the desk and stared at Macleish.

"Didn't you win a silver-digging in a crap game and then put it up in a poker deal with a certain gentleman?"

"Not me," said Younger Macleish.

"And didn't you lose the pot, and renege, and then cut out here to see if the digging was worth-while after all?"

"Not me," said Macleish.

"It was worth-while," said the gray-headed man.

"Well now," said Macleish.

"Sign this," said the gray-headed man softly, "and nobody reneged, and nobody's mad."

"I ain't mad," said Macleish. He rose suddenly.

The little gun swung to point steadily at him. Late, as usual, the beery man said a wordless *hup!* and his gun was out and, noisily, cocked. The loco-looking youth began to breathe loudly with his mouth open.

"Foot's asleep," said Macleish. He jiggled on it a couple of times and then sat down again.

After that nobody said anything until Brannegan got back.

The gray-headed man went back to his desk chair as Brannegan came in. Brannegan glanced at no one, but went straight to the desk and put down a packet of letters, a piece of polished rock crystal hanging from a fine gold chain, and a pincushion made like a little shepherdess with a full skirt. "Looky yere," said Brannegan. "He plays with dolls."

The gray-headed man was interested only in the letters. He fanned them and dealt them, one by one, picked up one and glanced through it, opened another and closed it right up again. He stacked them neatly and put them away from him next to the doll and the crystal pendant. Then he folded his long pale hands and seemed to close his eyes.

Macleish looked at the things on the desk and wondered if one or the other sister would get the pincushion and the pendant, or if it would be the schoolteacher after all.

The gray-headed man didn't move, but his sharp bright eyes were suddenly on Younger Macleish. "You're really just riding in, riding out."

"I told you," said Macleish.

The gray-headed man cursed. Coming from him, and coming as it did with such violence, the effect was like that matchflame a little earlier, which had made Macleish grunt.

"Mr. Brannegan," said the gray-headed man mildly, after he had his breath again, "We've got the wrong man."

Brannegan eyed Macleish with enmity, and said, "All that trouble."

To Macleish, the gray-headed man said, "Say you had a man to see, and you knew he was so good-looking he was practically pretty, and he'd dress so fancy he looked like a clown; and say you knew about him that he'd smoke the best cigars, call for the oldest brandy, and make for the nearest pretty face; and say you set up a trail he had to follow and an ambush he had to walk into. Then suppose just such a clown walked into it."

"I'd say you made a mistake," said Macleish.

"Just so, a mistake." Then he added, showing he was thinking, "A mistake." He sighed. "Mr. Brannegan, we've got to make it up to this young man."

"Sure," said Brannegan heavily.

"Return this man's property to him, Mr. Brannegan."

Brannegan got the things off the desk and gave Macleish his matches, his cigars, his poke, his letters, the crystal pendant. "That's awful pretty," he murmured as he gave Macleish the doll.

Macleish stowed the things in the various pockets of his fancy vest while the gray-headed man went on talking. He said, "I wouldn't want you to resent any of this, you know. An honest mistake. And I wouldn't want you to complain to the sheriff or anything like that. Not that it would make any difference. And I would be especially sad if you should talk about this to anyone you might meet on the trail." He stopped then, and waited.

Younger Macleish said, "I don't never complain."

"Oh fine," said the gray-headed man. Then he said it again, and, "I'd like to be sure of that. I really would."

Macleish shrugged at him. He couldn't think of anything to say.

The gray-headed man placed all the tips of all his fingers
together and stared at them mournfully, and said, "A long
and eventful life has taught me that there are after all only
three kinds of men. One kind gives his word and that's
enough. One kind, you pay, and that's enough. And one
kind needs a boot in the tail to show that you mean what
you say." He paused and said, without looking up, "I do
hope you are listening, Mr. Brannegan."

"Oh, every word," said Brannegan happily.

"Now then," said the gray-headed man, "I have his word.
Sort of. He said he doesn't complain. Well, I don't know
what kind of man he is, and I don't really care very much.
So we'll pay him, too. Give him twenty dollars, Mr. Brannegan."

"Give him *what?*" gasped the big man.

The gray-headed man thumbed a coin out of his watch
pocket and flipped it ringing across the desk. "Give it to
him."

"Well all right," said Brannegan, and took up the coin and
handed it to Macleish. Macleish took it and put it away.

"Now," said the gray-headed man, "take him outside and
give him a boot in the tail."

"I got just the one," said Brannegan. He came over to
Macleish, who stood up. Brannegan eyed him for a moment
and said over his shoulder, without looking, "Get your gun
out." Macleish heard the beery man's gun cocking and then
Brannegan got Macleish's left arm and twisted it behind
him, putting the fist tight up between Macleish's shoulder
blades. It hurt. He pulled Macleish off balance and ran him
out the door and along the gallery to the top of the stairs.

Here he gave him a shove outward and followed it with an accurate boot. Macleish spun floundering down the steps and brought up at the bottom, leaning against the newel post like a fence prop. Brannegan, incredibly, was right beside him, got the left fist between his shoulder blades again, and pulled him upright. Macleish looked up. The gray-headed man was leaning over the gallery rail, smiling slightly. Beside him, the youth stood, his mouth wide, tittering. At the head of the stairs stood the beery man, gun in hand. Brannegan ran Macleish the length of the bar and banged him out through the batwings. Macleish cleared the two low steps without touching, clipped the far edge of the duckwalk, and sprawled in the dust outside.

Behind the batwings, somebody yipped a shrill clear drag-rider's cattle-drive yip. A number of people helped make a bellow of laughter.

Macleish got to his feet. His face hurt. His hands and elbows hurt, and his left arm clear back to the shoulder bones hurt a whole lot. His fancy vest was a mess and he had a hole in the knee of his pants. He walked back to the hotel.

By the lamplight that streamed from the hotel, Macleish saw a man standing at the foot of the steps. It was the fat little old man from the livery. He had a white handkerchief pressed to his face. He said, "Oh, there you are. Gosh, son, a feller got to your saddle. I tried to stop him."

Macleish gently pulled the handkerchief down away from the old man's face. He had a puffy sort of hole on his cheekbone.

"Feller had a big ring," said the man from the livery. "I tried to stop him," he called apologetically as Macleish climbed the porch.

Some woman Macleish hadn't seen before was in the little lobby. She had a basin of water standing on the hotel desk. Miz Appleton was sitting behind the desk. The woman was dabbing at Miz Appleton's face with a wet clean cloth, and said to Macleish, "Oh, you must be the one. A man got to your things in your room."

Macleish stumped up the stairs, and as he reached the landing he heard Miz Appleton say, "I tried to stop him, Mr. Macleish."

Macleish went on upstairs. The door to his room was open. His saddlebags and spare clothes and blanket, and his Arbuckle coffee and trail bacon and beans were all dumped on the bed. He passed by with a glance and went to the wall peg where his gun-belt hung, and he took it down and strapped it on. He drew the gun, broke and spun it, clicked it straight and holstered it, and went back down the stairs. The women both spoke, but he didn't hear what they said.

He clumped down the duckwalks to the other hotel, looking straight ahead and not exactly hurrying. When he got there he kicked open the batwings and walked in. This time the piano and the faro games, as well as any talking and drinking and moving around that happened to be going on, really did stop, suddenly and altogether. Macleish paid no mind to anyone, but walked straight back to the stairs and went up them two at a time.

Somebody shouted then, but the sound was drowned out by the crash of the door as Macleish shouldered it half off its hinges and stood back.

He could see the desk and the lamp and the gray-headed man, his bright blue eyes all white-rimmed round. The man scooped open a drawer and Macleish drew and shot him through the right forearm and sprang inside.

The gray-headed man shrieked like a woman and curled up like a mealworm bit by a fire ant. Macleish stood in the center of the room, snapped a look to left, to the right. The beery man and the kid stood flat-footed by the end of the desk. Macleish made a motion with his gun and their hands went up as if they had been tied to the same string. Macleish slipped around behind them and got their guns. He threw the guns out through the draped window behind the desk.

He said, "Face the wall," and they were very brisk about doing it. The gray-headed man had fallen and was writhing on the floor behind the desk, crying. Macleish backed around there and booted him out in the open where he could see him. Then he pulled down a drape and put two straight chairs back to back and threw a couple of half-hitches around the uprights at one side. He said, "Come here," and the two gunmen turned uncertainly and came sheepishly across to him. "Sit," he said.

Back to back they sat down. Keeping his gun on them, Macleish circled them twice with the drape, binding them tight to the chairs and to each other. He didn't bother to tie the free end, but just tucked it into itself; it would hold for as long as he wanted it to. He put his gun down on the desk and placed one hand on the kid's face and one on the beery man's face, and whanged the backs of their heads together as hard as he could. When you crack one nut with another nut, practically every time only one of the two will break, and Macleish thought that that gave odds that neither one of these two deserved.

Macleish heard someone running, and he glanced at the

door and found it full of frightened faces. He waved his
gun at them and they disappeared. He jumped to the door
and flattened himself just inside. The running feet ceased
and became a deep growl: "Out o' my way!" and Brannegan exploded into the room just the way he himself had.
Macleish hit him alongside the head with his gun and he
threw out his arms and went forward to his hands and
knees, his head hanging. Macleish bent, hooked out his gun,
and sent it sailing through the window with one motion.
Then he got hold of Brannegan's left wrist, pulled the man
kneeling upright, and twisted the arm around and up,
meanwhile ramming his gun barrel into Brannegan's kidney.
"Up!" he said, and Brannegan stood up. Macleish walked
him through the door. There were people out there but
they made way.

Macleish brought Brannegan to the top of the stairs and
gave him a push and such a fine kick that everyone in the
place gasped, including Brannegan, who went out and
down like the front end of a rockslide. Macleish bounded
down after him and tried to stand him up with the bent-
arm thing, but Brannegan couldn't co-operate. Macleish
waved his gun and said to throw water on him.

"Yes, *sir!*" said the bartender, shuffling fast around the
end of the bar, bringing a big pitcher. Macleish, waiting,
moved gun and eyes all around. Everybody watched. Nobody moved.

The water made Brannegan twitch and groan. Macleish
snatched up Brannegan's ring hand and caught it between
his knees. Looking all around while he did it, he got the ring
off Brannegan's finger and put it on his own. The water
helped. Then he wrung Brannegan's left hand around behind him and told him "Up!"

Macleish walked him the length of the bar to the bat-wings, and then swung around to look at the people again. He didn't think any of them looked as if they wanted to stop him. Some followed him and Brannegan up to Miz Appleton's, but he didn't mind that.

He shoved Brannegan up the porch steps with his grip on the arm and also with the end of his gun. He hit the door with Brannegan and heard the latch break; he hadn't meant to do that. Miz Appleton and the other woman screamed.

"Is this the one?" he asked, and they screamed again. He dragged Brannegan to the door and let go his left arm and pulled his back hair until his face tipped up. Then he hit Brannegan with the ring on the cheekbone, and again on the chin sending him flying down into the crowd. Down there he saw the little old man from the livery, clasping his hands together over his fat stomach and jumping up and down in glee. He called him.

"Here," he said when the old man had climbed the porch. He handed him the ring. "Give this back to him."

"How?" asked the man, taking the ring and loving it.

"It's your deal," said Macleish, and went inside. He never did find out how the old man dealt it.

He slept well, and departed in the morning before Miz Appleton was up and about. He left her the gold twenty dollars he had been given the night before. In the livery, he liked the looks of his horse. Somebody had bothered to curry him. Macleish saddled up and went to buckling the bags and fixing the blanket roll, and by the time he was finished there was a bug-eyed stable boy yawning down from a little cubby in the mow, who said "Gosh."

"Gosh what?" asked Macleish.

"You're the fellow cleaned out the saloon last night, gosh."

"You tell the old feller," Macleish said, embarrassed, "my horse is happy anyhow. Got it?"

"Your horse is happy anyhow," nodded the boy. Macleish gave him money and mounted, and rode downstreet.

When he passed the other hotel, a woman called. "Mister."

He reined in. The girl with all the hair came running out into the middle of the street. She was all dun-colored in a cape and hood thrown over what was probably night clothes, and no makeup. She said, "I didn't know. I—I had to do what he said."

Macleish asked her, "Did you?" and rode on. He saw her lift her hand slowly and bite it.

A little way on, down where he hadn't been yet, a man called out to him and he stopped again. The man had a star pinned to his shirt. He said, "Look, I got two men bedded up back of the doctor's office, one with a broken arm and one with a cracked head. I got two more locked up in the jail."

Younger Macleish asked him, "Why?"

"Look, I can't hold them 'less you make a complaint."

"I don't complain." He lifted his hand to snap the lines and go, but the man said: "Look, were you thinkin' of maybe settlin' in hereabouts?"

"No," said Younger Macleish.

He rode out.

The Sheriff of Chayute

THEODORE STURGEON

The town came out of its houses, the propped-up weathered ones and the ones with the newly planted white pickets, out of the mercantile and the livery and even the Bat's Wing, and stood in the wide flat dusty street to watch the cloud in the southeast. They'd known for a week it would come, but it should have come yesterday, and they couldn't understand that. Billy Willow, who ran the mercantile, said so to the sheriff.

Ev Charger was the sheriff of Chayute, a gangly, ice-eyed man with the knack of keeping his heartbeat slow. He contemplated the cloud and couldn't understand either why it was a day late. "But anyhow, no use hopin' they won't come," he said, and with those words set himself like a clock, knowing what the message would have to be as the hours went by.

A lady stopped and called out from the duckboards: "You, Ev Charger, mind you keep a sharp eye on those—those ruffians. Chayute isn't what it was, and they'd best learn that. We will not tolerate—"

"Yes ma'am," the sheriff said evenly. From between Mrs. Finnan's bright china teeth, and out of her dried-apricot face, had come the same public speech a week ago, and this would be the eleventh time since. Billy said sharply, "Now,

Martha, when the sheriff comes into your place an' tells you
how much a yard to sell dimity, you've a right to tell him
how to run his business. Did he do that yet?"

Mrs. Finnan sniffed and did not respond to that, but
said, "A blessing when the railroad goes through," and
walked on. Charger wondered about that. The railroad
wouldn't come within forty miles of Chayute, and the
word had been around for years now that more and more
cattle were riding to market, arriving rested and soft. It
would mean the end of the big drives for sure. Chayute
would survive with farms and maybe the mine but it would
be a very different breed of town. Well it already was. Billy
was saying, "I'd be a devil's damfool to call that a blessing."
A cattle drive meant a lot to the mercantile and the saloon
and a couple other kinds of places, though a lot of the rest
would keep their doors open only out of a sort of defiance.
And given their druthers, half the houses in Chayute would
like to have boarded up their shutters or gophered clear
underground. Then "Priss," snapped Billy Willow, "you
come here."

The prettiest girl in town, yes and prettier than anything in the next four towns north and three east, stepped
off the duckboards and came to her daddy. Billy was a
laughter-beaten, weather-wrinkled little hickory stick of a
man, and for all his endless good nature, his kids obeyed
him in a way that would be the envy of a colonel in the
cavalry. Ev Charger was going to ask Billy one day how
that was done. "Yes, Daddy."

Billy peered into the glowing face. Priss Willow had
skin smooth as a new-blown magnolia and there's a western
tree called jacaranda which blooms a unique blue with

lavender in it: Priss Willow's eyes. "You got color on, girl?"

She got some then. "Oh no, Daddy."

Billy peered close again. "Well good then. Go help your maw."

"Yes, Daddy." She smiled shyly at the sheriff, which made him want to blink his eyes, and they watched her move away—a pleasure. She'd a way of moving unlike other folk, who just have to move up and down a little with each step. She did not.

Ev Charger thought to ask then and there, "How do you get your kids to mind you so, Billy? For sure it warn't with a willow switch."

"Oh, I ben known to wave one," said Billy, and laughed. Then he saw it was a straight question. Younguns grow yeast in their veins at a certain time, and the bubbles come in a lot of ways, not all of them good. The town had had its fair share of this in recent days as cattle became less to it and crops and the mine more, and they had to put a third room on the schoolhouse and those neat little pickets began to show along the street. Some of this yeasting became sheriff's business, and what to do was forever a puzzler.

Billy said, "No kid's a bad kid, whatever they say about blood. If you believe that, they know it and don't get bad. Only other thing you got to do is give 'em something that says 'thus far you can go, an' no farther.' It really don't make no difference what it is, you know. There's got to be a wall around 'em somewhere. Somepin for 'em to kick against. They call it a wall but they know it's a shelter." He came closer to talk privately, laughed again and said, "I don't give a hoot owl's holler if Priss powders up a bit, leastwise not more'n her maw does, but she don't know that."

They stood together watching the loom of the dust cloud

over the late-lit southwest hills. Charger knew from the talk
that they were both thinking the same thing, talking about
the same thing—in the middle of that cloud was a hard-
jawed kid name of Hank Shadd, yes and the old man who
had made him what he was. Nobody ever built a wall around
Hank, unless it was all those things that go to make a
man out of a boy. And it was Olman Shadd's idea of what
makes a man—that is, to know what you want and go for
it in straight lines. Two years ago they'd driven through here
and Hank had first seen Priss Willow. Last year he had first
seen her: a sizable difference; and she certainly saw him at
the same time, which was why the color on her face just
now, whether or not it was rouge pot or yeast.

Ev Charger knew the Shadds well and from way back.
Olman Shadd was only a loose handful of years older than
Charger, but even when Charger was a wet-eared calfling
they were calling Olman Shadd "the Old Man." Like a lot of
other lawmen of the time, Charger had cows in his history.
His first drive, and that was a long while back, had been
under Olman Shadd—and Shadd had already bossed four of
them, handling a crew of rannies older, and some bigger
than he was. You did what he said because he never gave
an order that didn't make sense; he knew his country and
his cows and his men. If you couldn't figure out the sense
you did it anyway, and right now, because he was a man
who would back up an order with fists or feet or bullets if
need be, no matter what, even "please pass the salt." Ev
Charger never ran afoul with him but once, and that was on
his first drive, when he had maybe more enthusiasm than
knowledge or care, and one night tiredly hobbled his roan
with a granny knot. It took him forty daylight minutes to
catch his mount the next morning, and the Old Man waved

him up from where he had been riding flank—a real kindness to an apprentice. "Ride drag," was all the Old Man said, and young Ev dropped back and for five days drank dust with his nostrils and chewed it with his eyelids and spat it out in gritty tears, wading through cowflop the whole time, and contemplating the craft of carefulness.

He saw the shape and place of the cloud and said to Billy Willow, "They'll be camping by the ford and they should have the cows put to bed by just past sundown. Reckon they'll blow in about nine o'clock."

Yes, nine o'clock, full dark, thirsty and all the rest that goes with it—and it was Shadd's way to make up for a tight rein by discarding bridle and bit when the time came. "It'll be a noisy night," said Billy Willow, with absolute understanding, and went to see to his store.

And it was ten after nine in the darkening town when they first heard the gunshots—pinpricks of sound lengthening into crooked-y hollow tubes of it, laying out along the echoing foothills, yes, and hoofbeats and a lot of idiot yipping. Ev Charger came out of his office and walked quietly up the boards to the Bat's Wing, while the townsfolk popped out of their doors to listen and back in again to hide, like a whole row of those wooden cuckoos on a Bavarian clock. Charger stepped out into the street and hung one of his shoulderblades on the high hitching rail in front of the Bat's Wing Saloon and waited. Shadd's men raced in in a sort of barely controlled stampede, probably because of some brainless poke's wager about the last man buying the first drink. That game somehow got lost at the sight of the sheriff, though all he did was get his shoulder off the rail and stand up straight.

He looked up at them and nodded. "Howdy, Shadd."

The Old Man reined close but didn't begin to dismount. A mounted man has special advantages. His view is better and his range is wider and it's natural (except for a smooth-bore bird-killer) to shoot straight or down rather than up-wards. But most of all, he's looking down on you, specially if he's slab-jawed, grizzled, cold-eyed Olman Shadd. "Howdy, Ev," he said in a voice like granite sliding on granite. He called the sheriff by his name, which was a kindness, for after losing his horse that time Ev Charger had been known as Granny for a hard-fought season.

Charger looked around at the others. Some he knew, had ridden with 'way back. Billy Oats was there, face blow-torched and hair frosted by the years, Injun John, Juice Jaw (Did he ever have another name? Awake or asleep he carried a great bulge of tobacco-cud in one side of his face, and he had a whole vocabulary of spits), Neil was there, absolutely untouched by all those years, and Adams who had taught him that when you point your finger at some-thing, even over your shoulder or behind your back, you do it with surprising accuracy, so that if you lay your index finger along the barrel of your gun and point, you can shoot off the back doorknob of a barroom from a batwing door-way. And tight-lipped young Hank Shadd, of course, look-ing for someone. Then there were some more men he didn't know, and didn't have to, really, to understand that they were the same hard riders, hard drinkers, and hardnosed brawlers as the rest. "Howdy, boys. Juicy. Neil. Hey Injun. Billy . . ." They grunted their greetings. Juicy spat pleas-ure. Then Charger added, "I'll want your guns."

It got very quiet. But for the half-lathered horses, it got

so quiet for so long that Charger had the crazy idea that nobody would move or say a word at all forever and ever. And the funny thing was, nobody looked at him. They were all looking at Old Man Shadd. Looking to him.

Shadd said, "What's that you say?" So the sheriff said it again.

"Why is that, Ev?" the Old Man asked too quietly.

Juicy spat wonderment.

"It's the law," said Charger. "Nobody totes iron here after sundown."

"Wasn't so last year," said Shadd.

"Right, sir. Town ordinance. You want to see the book?"

"No I don't want to see the book. Take your word." A sudden something lit up Shadd's steady eyes. Juicy recognized it for what it was, and spat fury. Shadd thumbed a dollar out of his Levi's and flicked it ringing into the air and caught it. "Tell you what I'll do, so we don't git into no outnumbered argymint here. You call it, Sheriff, and if you win the toss we'll do as you say."

"Mister Shadd," said Charger, because if Shadd had to call him Sheriff, he had to call Shadd Mister. "Mister Shadd, I am just telling you what the law is here. Now a law that rests on the turn of a dollar is no law at all, so I cain't play it like that."

Shadd's nostrils expanded a whole lot and from them there issued a sharp strong hiss. Charger knew that one well. So did Juicy, who spat danger. The sheriff held tight until he saw Shadd's mouth open to say the one word that would commit everyone to one course or the other, and then cut in swiftly but softly: "Why tote guns? Ain't you-all the match for unarmed townsfolk without 'em?" But he smiled a little while he said it.

Shadd exploded with a roar—it was a tense two seconds before anyone could be sure that the noise was laughter. He was not laughing so much at the ludicrous picture the sheriff had conjured up as at the ingenuity of the trap Charger had set for him. With a suddenness that made the sheriff's gun-hand cramp, Shadd clapped his hand to his belt . . . unbuckled it, handed it down. And before he collected the others, Charger unbuckled his own. Juicy spat wonderment.

"Have a good time," said Charger, mounting the walk with his load of belts.

It was a noisy night. Before it was done everyone hated Ev Charger—or so he thought. Mrs. Finnan sent word for him to come see her right now, and what crazy idea he had in his head about her and one of Shadd's men he wouldn't admit even to himself. But she was safe and sound, bolted snug inside her darkened drygoods, peering out to look for him. When he came she shot the bolt back, spun him inside and whipped the door to again as if the invaders were not men but a grasshopper plague. "You've got to stop it," she said angrily.

"Stop what?"

"All that noise in the saloon."

"Noise, Miz Finnan?"

"And cursing and swearing."

"What they been saying, Miz Finnan?"

"You know I wouldn't repeat any of it!"

"'Course not," said the sheriff. "I just wanted to be sure you heard anything."

"You know trail-riders!"

"Yep. Ma'am: Just what did you hear?"

"They were singing," she said defiantly.

He concentrated very hard on his hat, which his hands were turning round and round without really being told to. He said, "Miz Finnan, a trail rider is up an' around before the sun is. He finds his horse in the dark an' most usually he's got three hours' hard work before he gets so much as a mug o' coffee. Whatever's lost he finds. Whatever's busted he fixes. He cain't be everywhere at once but he tries. He rides when it's wet, when it's cold, when it's both at once an' muddy to boot. He eats dust an' everything in the world smells of cow, an' he don't get to town much at all. An' when he does, are you goin' to begrudge him singin' a song?

None of his words were angry words but apparently his tone of voice betrayed him. He hadn't shouted but she quailed as if he had, and then marched to the door and snapped it open. "You're as bad as they are, Ev Charger. You used to be one of them and you still are." He went out and walked back up the street. He had a funny thought: folks sometimes said "the face of the city," in the papers or a book. He'd never thought of Chayute having a face, and he wondered now if its face looked like Martha Finnan's. If it did it was mad at him, and not in any way he could do anything about.

His office was next door to the doctor's. The doctor had the only place in town with a doorway set back from the walk, and someone was in the doorway. It wasn't the doctor because the place was dark. Charger paused and heard a couple of people talking quietly. It was a weird way of talking:

Priss Willow's soft smooth voice: "I had five whole years of schoolin' already, and I'll get two more at least."

Hank Shadd, with his father's grate already begun, but overlaid with unsureness, shyness: "I didn't exactly get shot. I got powder burns all over my hand."

"Maw says my apple pie's as good as hers. She says if I get the trick with the crust it'll be better."

"Woke up in the first light, there's this diamondback not two feet away."

"I could become a dressmaker too, if I wanted. But I druther—no I won't tell you that."

"Wasn't coiled up yet so I knew I c'd git to him before that first strike. So I grabbed him right behind the head."

"Maw says I should be a schoolteacher. She says schoolteachers git the best kind of husbands."

"Helt him to the ground with the one hand, got m'gun with th'other, blowed his head off."

"Daddy'd like that too, but he just likes the idea of me teachin'."

"Burnt m'hand, scared h—— uh, beg pardon, scared the boys half out of their skin and my dad too."

Charger went quietly into his office without bothering them, and wagging his head. Priss a-rambling on one line, Hank on another, and both of them doubtless thinking something else. He remembered something Billy once said: "Don't never listen to a word folks say, Ev—listen to what they mean."

He took a medicinal shot from the quart in his bottom drawer, thinking a little wistfully what it was like in the saloon, not that they'd mind if he walked in, but it couldn't be the same. He started out. He didn't mean to be extra quiet, or maybe he did.

"They're sayin' it'll all be Herefords and the longhorn's on the way out."

"It was blue with little gores here and some lace."

"Hereford don't even look like a beef. Like a oversize dog."

"Took off the sleeves and put in darts so they'd puff way out."

"Ride in steam cars like a dude."

What that really is, Charger thought as he moved up-street, is railway talk. The two rails don't ever meet either, but they get along together just fine.

Then he began to run. The noise he heard wasn't a loud one, and he barely heard it at all what with the bumbling roar issuing from the saloon. It was one short syllable, but the kind of forced, sharp sound that means trouble.

He ran past the saloon and up to the livery. In the dark mouth of the entrance was a flicker of movement, and hard breathing. Two figures were locked together back there in the spilled hay, and as Charger slid to a halt one of them —Barney, the livery's owner—broke free and dived toward him. No, not to him, but to the shelf over the bill table. He reached between two account books and his hand came out with a gun in it. He whirled toward the other man, who was on his feet ready to rush.

Charger had a hard arm around Barney's throat and the other hand on his gun wrist before anyone, including the sheriff, knew he had moved. "Drop it, Barney. Drop it!"

"I'll kill the—"

"The hell you will." Charger gave a sudden surge, bent the elbow, surprisingly released the grip across Barney's neck and used the freed hand to take the gun.

The other man was one of Shadd's riders, one that Charger didn't know. He was a tall thin one, round-shouldered and gaunt, and he was wall-eyed mad. Not so much that he couldn't check himself, though. "What's this about?"

"Come in here an' found him stealin'."

The gaunt man took a leaping pace nearer—but stopped. "You're a stinkin' liar," he said, and knocked wet off his chin with the back of his hand. He spoke to Ev: "I come in here and knocked and hollered and there wasn't nobody. All I wanted was oats for my hoss, he hasn't had good grazing in three days now. An' this bastard comes out of no place and licks me with a ax-handle."

Charger didn't believe him. With total enthusiasm he did not believe him. On the other hand who was to prove the truth? And if Barney came by for a look and saw a stranger fanning through the back bins, who could blame him? But then—he wasn't going to think of what would have happened in Chayute that night if a town man had shot a rider he himself had disarmed.

"You get on back to the saloon," he told the rider. "Barney, you'll get your gun back in the mornin'. No guns after sundown means you too."

They both opened their mouths to protest, looked at each other and then at Charger, who wasn't holding the gun on them but sure hadn't put it away. The rider spat near their feet and went on back to the saloon.

"You shouldn'ta gone for this, Barney."

"Guess you're right, Ev, but what would *you* do?"

Charger grinned briefly. "Same thing." He clapped Barney's shoulder and went out. A running man half-knocked him off his feet. "Billy, f'God's—"

This was a Billy Willow he'd never seen before, out of

breath, frantic. He clutched at Charger's leather vest. "Priss's gone!"

"Now you jus' git yourself together an' come along with me."

Billy began to shout. "I didn't raise that girl to run with the likes of that sprat of Olman Shadd's. I tell you he's going to deal with me, I'll see to it he never fouls my nest or anyone else's. He—"

"Now hush," said Charger, but it didn't work, or not soon enough. Three Shadd men had been drawn out of the saloon by the ruckus, and one of them was the Old Man himself.

"I'll handle it," Charger said as he propelled Willow on by. It came out like a warning.

"'Likes of that sprat of Olman Shadd's'?" The Old Man turned to a rider. "You hear something like that?"

It was Juicy, who spat yes.

Charger pointed into the doctor's doorway. "There you go, Billy." And immediately there emerged a frightened Priss and a lowering Hank. Charger flicked a glance behind him. The three had followed them, and more besides.

Billy Willow snatched the girl by the shoulders and whirled her half around. "You git yourself home and go to your room. I'll deal with you later." With a terrified look at Hank, the girl fled. Billy whirled on the blinking boy. "As for you, you rotten randy little goat, you'll stay away from my Priss or you'll answer to me. If ever I see you—"

"Stop right there, Billy," Charger said coldly. He had never in his life spoken to this wise, happy little man like this, but then it was a Billy he'd never seen before.

Then the Old Man was there like a tidal wave curling and about to break. To Billy he grated, "He really ain't good enough for her, that it? Well let me tell you something, he don't need to sniff around any pasty-faced, bandy-legged—"

"You too, Shadd," snapped Charger, and found himself immensely astonished. "Anything you say now you'll wish you hadn't in the mornin' an' you both know it."

Young Hank Shadd spoke up. "I'm here to tell you I never—" and as if the same string had pulled them the sheriff and both fathers told him to shut his mouth. And that was the end of it until the next afternoon, for after one more sullen round, the riders picked up their weapons and left town.

Charger was in his office poring over the county chart when the kid ran in with the bad news. The sheriff had been at it for an hour and a half—he didn't really know why. Maybe it was because of the trail-riders last night. Nobody but a damn' fool stays with the trails year after year —which is why every drive had its share of damn' fools— but like railroading or going to sea or some other things you never did quite get all the grit pumped out of your blood. Charger liked where he was and what he was doing, but all the same some small part of him went jingling out with them to the smell of cow and the brainless bawling, and the good ache of a long hard day, and trail food sauced by a real working man's appetite.

His finger traced the old trail up from the lush land to the southwest which had bred the herd. He knew those hills, and that alkali patch—twice he'd had stampede crossing that, when the steers smelt the waterhole. Yonder was the place he picked off a cougar with one shot, and saved a calf. Over there the ford that was flooded when they got to it, and still they beat across and lost only seven head.

And here the black new marks on the chart, the rail line. Crews had pioneered the roadbed last summer and would have the rails in this year, and that would be about the end of the old trail. They'd brought in powder gangs and blasted through a hogback—now that would've been a blessing back in his day. Look how the trail had to wind, better than forty miles around. Now you could drive your steers straight through and save a day, or would until the rails were in.

Save a day. Days were money. Shadd had lost a day, somewhere.

Somewhere? Right there! He put his finger on the place. Old Man Shadd had unaccountably crossed the railroad right-of-way and kept with the long looping old trail, instead of cutting through. You'd think he'd jump at the chance to use the new road, after what the new road was doing to the old ways he was so hitched to.

Charger was wagging his head in puzzlement over this when the kid burst in. "Mister Kelly says Hank Shadd is in the saloon, he's been drinkin' and workin' up a mad."

The whole thing came to Charger in a single blaze. Once he had been inside the skin of a lad like that, and he knew —he knew as if he had been through last night and this morning, every second of it, along with Hank Shadd. Aggrieved, insulted, called names and told to shut up . . . yes, and in love to boot; and with "be a man" as his weaning-pap, every day of his life until now. Only nobody really ever told him how. So the kidding, the new name—what would they call him? Randy? Billy goat? Probably he had to fight a couple of them last night and this morning. And the Old Man wouldn't be much help. "Ride drag," is all he'd say. Yes, and back he'd go, and he'd be mad, and he'd think of a flower-face and let the beef clatter past him, stay behind, ride to town, try to be a man by drinking up his mad.

Charger snatched up his gun-belt and ran, strapping it around him. He knew where to go—the mercantile. He stopped near it to knot the thong around his thigh, and by the time he straightened up there was Hank Shadd, mounted and sitting too straight. Charger called him but he wouldn't hear. Hank ranged up before the mercantile and called out in a choked voice, "Willow!"

Billy Willow's head appeared at the door and popped back again.

"Send her out, Willow. I got something to say to her."

An upstairs window swung open and there was the magnolia face, crinkled, the jacaranda eyes horrified. And Billy Willow stamped out on the duckboards, a graying bantam—Billy with a gun-belt on!

"She has nothing to say to you. Now git."

"She's coming out or I'm comin' in." He stepped his horse a pace closer.

Billy hung his hand over his holster. His voice was thick, and the veins at the sides of his neck stood out like fenceposts. "Try gettin' past me an' you're dead."

Upstreet, the sound of hooves galloping in.

The window above was empty.

"If that's really it, then," said the boy, and went for his gun. There was a hoarse grating shout just behind Charger, but he paid it no mind. He drew and shot Hank Shadd out of his saddle. He put away his gun before he turned and saw the Old Man spring down from a wheezing mount and run to the boy. He wasn't there ahead of Priss Willow, though. The girl was down beside him, his head in her lap, and she had a fine proud glare of disgust for Ev Charger and all the world besides.

Shadd knelt briefly by the wounded man and then stood up and turned to face the sheriff.

"Shoulder," he said. And he said to the girl, "Will you watch over him?"

She put her arms around Hank's head. Behind her, Ev could see a shocked-sober Billy Willow raise his hands and drop them in defeat. Then he grinned a little—thank the Powers, Billy Willow's own old smile. He came over to where Charger and the Old Man were standing and though nobody asked him, he said, "I sent her off to bed and it's the first time she ever disobeyed me, she slipped away to talk to him there in the doorway but I didn't know where she was."

Nobody asked Shadd to explain either, but he said, "Made him ride drag. Don't know why I thought to come back and look, but he was gone and I knowed he'd come here."

Charger knew that was as far as either would ever go in the way of apology. He said, "You raise a young'un to mind you, and one day he don't, why, it must be pretty important."

They all looked at the young couple. The doctor had come out. The Old Man said, "He's in good hands. I'll be by after the drive."

He mounted his horse and looked down on them. "Hey, Ev," he said. "I knew we could make it be just like old times, a shootin' an' everything, and that sheriff we was always lookin' for, that would back up one of my boys." Then he smiled: it was the first Ev Charger had ever seen on that face. He said something that explained why he had taken the old trail and scorned the bright easy scar of the railroad right-of-way. "I knew we could do it—one more time."

"I'll buy you a drink," said Billy Willow, and did, and for the traildrivers, that was the last of the good old days.